EXCITEMENT, SUSPENSE—AND KAY TRACEY—GO TOGETHER!

Sixteen-year-old Kay Tracey is an amateur detective with a sense of sleuthing that a professional might envy. Her closest friends who share her adventures are Betty Worth and her twin sister Wendy. Whenever there is a mystery in the small town of Brantwood, you'll find Kay and her two friends in the middle of it.

If you like spine-tingling action and heart-stopping suspense, follow the trail of Kay and her friends in the other books in this series: *In the Sunken Garden, The Six Fingered Glove Mystery, The Mansion of Secrets, The Green Cameo Mystery* and *The Message in the Sand Dunes*.

Bantam Books by Frances K. Judd
Ask your bookseller for the books you have missed

THE DOUBLE DISGUISE
IN THE SUNKEN GARDEN
THE SIX FINGERED GLOVE MYSTERY
THE MANSION OF SECRETS
THE GREEN CAMEO MYSTERY
THE MESSAGE IN THE SAND DUNES

A Kay Tracey Mystery

THE DOUBLE DISGUISE

Frances K. Judd

A BANTAM SKYLARK BOOK

THE DOUBLE DISGUISE

*A Bantam Skylark Book/published by arrangement with
Lamplight Publishing, Inc.*

PRINTING HISTORY

*Hardcover edition published in 1978 exclusively by Lamplight
Publishing, Inc.*
Bantam Skylark edition/October 1980

*Bantam Books are published by Bantam Books, Inc. Its trade-
mark, consisting of the words "Bantam Books" and the por-
trayal of a bantam, is Registered in U.S. Patent and Trademark
Office and in other countries. Marca Registrada. Bantam Books, Inc.,
666 Fifth Avenue, New York, New York 10103.*

PRINTED IN THE UNITED STATES OF AMERICA

0 9 8 7 6 5 4 3 2 1

BOOK DESIGNED BY MIERRE

Contents

THE DOUBLE
DISGUISE

Horses, sleigh, and driver had plunged over
the cliff!

I

The Stranger

"This snow is fantastic!" exclaimed Kay Tracey, as she got off the train at Brantwood.

Suddenly Kay was rudely shoved. Turning quickly, she saw a young man pushing his way through the milling crowd toward a middle-aged woman.

Kay was thinking that the man could at least have said excuse me when her thoughts were interrupted by her friend Betty Worth.

"No school Friday! We can spend the week-end sledding and skating," said Betty.

"Brr!" shivered Betty's twin sister Wendy. "This is the kind of weather I like to spend indoors by a cozy open fire with a good book."

The Worth twins were not in the least alike. Betty, was fair-haired and very lively while Wendy was dark-haired and serious. Both were alike in one thing, however; their close friendship with Kay. Kay was a slender, attractive girl with thick, curly brown hair. She was friendly, sincere, and very popular in the nearby high school which she and her friends commuted to from the little town of Brantwood.

As the girls made their way across the train platform Kay saw the woman she had noticed moments before tumble to the pavement. Her purse flew open and all its contents spilled out. Her suitcase also snapped open and its contents, too, were strewn over the snow.

Kay and the twins rushed up to help the stunned woman but were brushed aside by the man who had bumped into Kay earlier. He assumed charge of the woman's things in a possessive manner. He was short, slender, very blonde, with a rosy complexion.

Kay picked the woman's purse up from the snow and was about to brush it off when this young man snatched it from her almost as if he suspected her of trying to steal it.

"Just a minute, please!" said Kay; "I am just trying to help this lady. By the way, may I ask why you are taking charge of her things?"

"I'm her son!" retorted the young man unpleasantly and went on hastily collecting the things which had burst from the suitcase.

In the meantime the twins were helping the woman to sit up.

"Do you think you can walk?" asked Kay, stooping over to extend a helping hand.

"Perhaps you had better rest awhile inside the station," added Wendy.

"You are very kind," murmured the woman, struggling to rise. By leaning on the girls' arms she made her way, limping, into the warmth of the building, and sank down on a bench.

"Thank you so much!" she breathed, her voice low and gentle.

She leaned back and closed her eyes, her face as white as the snow which covered her from head to foot. Kay noted the lady's well-bred accents and her expensive and tasteful clothes. At that moment she opened her eyes and a little color drained back into her cheeks.

"My purse and my suitcase!" she cried anxiously.

She tried to get up, but sank back, feeling faint, and shut her eyes again.

"Your son has them," Kay said reassuringly. "Don't worry about them. He'll bring everything in as soon as he's got it all collected. In the meantime I'll get you some water."

Kay hurried to the water fountain while Betty dashed out to get a taxi. Wendy stood by brushing off the melting snow. Suddenly the woman looked up at her and asked, "Who did she say has my things?"

"Your son," said Wendy.

"My son!" the lady exclaimed sharply. "Why, I have no son! My name is Miss Alice Janey, and I'm quite alone in the world and have been since my dear father died. I don't know what you're talking about!"

"The young man who was picking up your things told us he was your son, didn't he, Kay?" asked Wendy as her friend returned with the water.

"Oh, dear me!" cried the lady in distress. "He's a thief! What has he done with my bag? I must get it back; as it contains valuables!"

Kay rushed out to look for the young man, but he was nowhere to be seen! The lady, greatly disturbed, tried to go to the door, but her faintness returned and she slumped back on the bench.

At that moment Chris Eaton, an unpleasant girl who attended the girls' high school shoved her way through the gathering crowd until she reached Miss Janey.

"You must lie down at once while I call a doctor!" Chris announced.

In her bossy fashion, Chris immediately started giving orders. She commanded the curious crowd to stand back, and persistently pushed Miss Janey down on the bench. When Kay returned, Miss Janey, annoyed at Chris addressed herself to Kay.

"I have been robbed! You must get a policeman and catch that man!" she exclaimed.

Dashing out again, Kay bumped into Betty who had not been able to find a taxi. She mentioned that she'd seen the lady's son hurry up the street with the bags.

Racing in the direction Betty pointed, Kay was nearly run down by a car which skidded to a halt with a shrill scream of brakes.

"Watch where you're going!" a man yelled from the car window.

Kay looked up to see her cousin, Bill Tracey. Bill was a young lawyer and had shared the Tracey home and its responsibilities since the death of Kay's father. There was nobody Kay would rather have seen at that particular moment!

Breathlessly she poured out the situation to him as she scrambled into his car. Bill lost no time in speeding after the stranger.

"There he is!" exclaimed Kay as she caught sight of the hurrying figure with Miss Janey's suitcase.

Bill sped ahead, only to be stopped by a traffic jam at a cross street. Meanwhile the stranger hurried on. As soon as he could Bill inched forward but the sharp squeal of a whistle and a traffic officer's forbidding hand stopped him.

Bill leaned out of his car and shouted, "Officer, we need your help. We're following a man who's running away with a stolen suitcase!"

The officer hopped inside the car and Bill sped along. The thief could still be seen in the distance but suddenly he took a quick turn and vanished.

"Maybe he stepped into that dingy car which shot out from a side street," suggested Kay.

Its license plate was too encrusted with snow to be readable, but a blonde head seemed faintly discernible from the window as the car darted away. Bill, Kay and the officer tried to follow him but finally they turned back in disappointment.

They returned to the station where the twins were sitting with Miss Janey. Bill and the officer questioned her and learned that the man who had posed as her son had made away with the contents of her safe deposit box. She was about to transfer her valuables and certain confidential papers to a bank in Brantwood where she was planning to live.

"I used to visit here when I was a girl," she explained. "As my home is now broken up and it is necessary for me to economize, I plan to settle in Brantwood where I used to be happy. I want to try to complete some work that my late dear father and I were interested in. But now, I don't know what I'll do." Her pale lips trembled.

The policeman said cheerily, "Don't worry, Madam, we'll catch that thief and get your valuables back for you."

Despite this reassurance, Miss Janey turned chalk white and fainted away.

II

A Chase

As Miss Janey collapsed, Kay caught her and eased her down onto the bench.

Chris, delighted at the excitement, ran for another cup of water. However, in her eagerness to be the one to revive Miss Janey, she squeezed the paper cup too hard and the water spurted all over the poor woman's face and trickled down her neck.

"A big help you are, Chris," commented Betty, mopping up the ice water with her handkerchief.

The splash, though clumsy had proved effective. Miss Janey's eyelids fluttered and she looked up at the faces bending over her.

"I'm sorry!" she sighed. "Please help me get to the hotel. I'll be all right if I can just get some rest after this shock."

"We won't have you going to a hotel," declared Kay emphatically. "You're going straight home with me. My mother is getting our guest room ready for you this very minute! Come, Miss Janey, my cousin will take us home."

Despite her protests, Miss Janey soon found herself in the rear seat of Bill's car, supported on either side by a twin. In a short time they were turning into the Tracey driveway.

Mrs. Tracey was waiting for them at the door. Before Kay could introduce the two women, Miss Janey cried, "Kathryn! I can't believe my eyes! After all these years! What a coincidence!"

"Alice Janey! Is it really you? Why, you haven't changed a bit!"

The two girlhood friends fell into each other's arms, as the girls and Bill stood staring in amazement.

"Come, Alice, let me get you settled in your room. The girls will bring you something hot to drink. Then we can talk."

When at last Miss Janey was snug in bed, sipping hot tea, the twins and Kay told Mrs. Tracey all about the robbery.

"That thief was rather good-looking," ventured Betty.

"Too sissy!" Kay said. "I'm surprised he had the nerve to carry out a robbery."

"It just goes to show that one should never judge by appearances," Mrs. Tracey commented.

"Oh, I hope they catch him!" Miss Janey murmured in despair.

"He'll be caught if we have to do it ourselves!" Kay declared so seriously that their anxious guest had to smile.

"If Kay makes up her mind to catch him, you can be sure she will!" Mrs. Tracey remarked. "It is getting to be a habit with her!"

She described some of the detective work which Kay, with the help of the twins, had carried out on former occasions. It all began with a local mystery which nobody in Brantwood had been able to solve. Finding several clues, Kay had eventually come up with the answer to the puzzling case. From that time on, people came to Kay with difficult cases.

"Solving mysteries is the greatest fun in the world," declared Kay enthusiastically. "And now, if we are to work out yours, we'll have to know more about what happened and what was stolen."

"To begin with," Miss Janey answered, "I was nervous about carrying the contents of my safe deposit box with me on the train. I suppose I shouldn't have done it. There were papers of father's, however, that I hated to trust to anyone else or even to the mails. I thought an ordinary suitcase would arouse no suspicion of its valuable contents. I cannot understand how it burst open so easily when I fell."

"How did you fall?" Kay asked.

"At the time it seemed a plain case of slipping on the snow," Miss Janey continued, "but I do remember being shoved roughly. It was probably done on purpose. I'm afraid it is all part of a well-laid plan. The idea that I am the victim of a plot terrifies me!"

"If that's the case, the sooner we get to the bottom of it the better!" cried Kay. "I'm convinced the thief made his getaway in that car. There was snow on the license plates so nobody could read them but I'm certain I've seen that car from time to time on the old river road. What do you say," she asked, turning to the twins, "shall we take a ride up that way?"

"Sure!" agreed Betty, springing from her chair.

"That road is so desolate," said Wendy, but seeing Kay and Betty's enthusiasm she decided to go along.

Within minutes Kay had the family car out on the

road and the trio were on their way. They had been breezing along for some time when the car gave a discouraging cough and began to slow down.

"What's the matter?" Wendy asked, uneasily.

"Out of gasoline!" Kay moaned as the car came to a standstill.

"We're miles from a station," Betty said.

"Half a mile only," Kay corrected, hopping out. "Come on, Betty, we'll go back and get gas. Wendy, you stay here in the car."

Trudging through the snow to the station and then back again with the heavy gas can was exhausting for the two girls. They were relieved to get back to the car. Putting the container can on the road, Kay unscrewed the cap of her empty gas tank.

At that moment a car sped down the road, swishing snow on either side.

"Watch out! That driver's crazy!" cautioned Kay sharply.

Betty hastily skipped out of the way just in time to be missed by the same car with the snow-covered license plates! It whizzed by in a flash.

In jumping to safety, Betty had abandoned the gas can in the road, close to the side of the Tracey car. The reckless driver barely missed hitting the car itself, but had run over and flattened the container. The fuel now was running out in a puddle in the snow.

"Oh no!" cried Wendy.

"Never mind, we were lucky not to be hit!" consoled Betty, shaky from her narrow escape.

"Did you see the driver?" asked Kay. "It was the thief who stole Mrs. Janey's suitcase!"

"How maddening that he spilled our gas!" Betty stormed.

"I'll say!" Kay raged. "We'll have to go back for more."

"Don't leave me alone this time," Wendy objected, leaping out of the car to join the other two.

Three crestfallen girls began the long, cold hike back to the gas station.

"There's Chris Eaton getting air in her tires," Betty cried. "Hi, Chris, we're stranded down the road. How about giving us a lift back there, with some gas to start our car?"

Chris greeted the girls frostily. "Sorry, but I don't have time now," she answered.

"If that isn't exactly like her!" fumed Betty in disgust, as Chris backed her car onto the road.

As she did so, a big black car roared down the road at breakneck speed. Chris, on the wrong side of the road, backed directly into the path of the on-rushing car.

Realizing what was happening, Chris tried desperately to get out of the way before being hit but her wheels spun futilely in the snow and then her engine stalled! With a blast of the horn, the shriek of brakes and a loud crash, the black car smashed into Chris's.

III

Women of Mystery

Chris's scream tore the air. Wendy hid her face in her hands. Kay and Betty ran over to Chris certain that she had not been hurt because of the lively way she was shouting at the two men who had crashed into her.

"Why don't you look where you're going? Why do you drive at such a crazy speed? I'll sue you for this!" she shrieked in fury.

"You backed right in front of us, Miss, and you were on the wrong side of the road!" answered one of the men from the other car.

"I'll see that you're charged with reckless driving!" Chris raged.

"We're chasing a thief," explained the second man, getting out of the car.

Then Chris saw that they were policemen.

"That man passed us earlier, going like the wind," Kay informed the men.

"He nearly ran over us down the road where our car is stranded. We're out of gas," Betty added.

"Jump in with us and we'll drop you off at your car. You can show us which way that thief went," said one of the officers.

The girls hastily piled in, deserting Chris. In no time they were at their own vehicle. The police car stopped for the girls to jump out, then whizzed away.

Kay carefully poured the second can of gas into the tank, then drove back to the station to fill up before returning home. Chris was still there, arranging for repairs to her car. Kay goodnaturedly offered her a ride back to town. The invitation was accepted glumly.

Kay drove her friends home and reached her own house just in time for supper. She was glad of the opportunity to talk again with Miss Janey. By this time the woman was much clearer about the whole situation.

"I just remembered something," she confided to Kay. "When I was at the bank arranging to get everything out of my safe deposit box there was a young woman who seemed awfully interested in what I was doing. She struck up a conversation with me while I was waiting and was quite inquisitive. I may have said something to her, in a general way, about my plans, in answer to her many questions."

"Can you remember anything you said?"

"Let me see. I think I mentioned Brantwood because she seemed to know the place and said it was such a pretty town. She asked where I was going to live, saying she had a relative here and was familiar with some of the streets."

"I hope you didn't tell her," Kay said.

Miss Janey looked worried. "No, I don't think so. I may have mentioned that I had bought a house. The young woman just seemed to worm things out of me against my will. At the time I thought she was a harmless, talkative girl. Now I'm not so sure."

"It sounds to me like she was trying to find out your plans," remarked Kay.

"I am afraid so," the woman confessed.

"What did she look like?" Kay asked curiously.

"I don't really remember. I didn't pay much attention to her," replied Miss Janey regretfully.

"You don't remember anything about the way she looked?" Kay urged.

Miss Janey pressed her fingers to her eyes and made an effort to bring to her mind an image of the young woman.

"Well, she was blonde; I remember that. Rather curly hair. She was dressed plainly in something dark. There was nothing distinguished about her. I'm not sure I would even recognize her if I saw her again."

"Was she taller than you?" Kay prompted.

"She was medium height and slender. I think she had on black gloves. I'm fairly sure that her coat was black and tailored looking. Yes, things are beginning to come back to me now. She wore a little face veil and that is probably why her features are not clear to me. She was rather well dressed, though not conspicuously."

Kay was busy scribbling these details in a little notebook. Now she looked up to say: "You're sure she was blonde?"

"Yes, quite sure."

"Maybe she's related to the blonde thief."

"Do you think so?" Miss Janey asked nervously.

"I have a hunch she was. The two probably plotted to steal your things after the young woman had found out what you were carrying and where you were going."

• 15 •

"I thought so little about her at the time, and now I find out she was probably the thief's accomplice!" Miss Janey sighed.

"I've tired you!" Kay cried. "You must get some rest. We can go into the whole thing in more detail tomorrow morning."

Long after everyone settled down for the night and the town clock had struck midnight, the telephone rang. Mrs. Tracey funbled for her slippers and robe, then pattered down the hall to answer it.

"Maybe they caught the thief," thought Kay, who had awakened also.

However, it was soon clear that this was not the reason for the call.

"Who is this?" demanded Mrs. Tracey sleepily. All she heard in response was a harsh crackling sound. "What's that? Who? Oh, he has hung up!"

"Who was it?" Kay asked, hurrying to her mother's side.

"Someone just threatened us. He said that if we meddle in this theft we'll be in great danger! Oh dear, what shall we do? I'll ask Bill's advice," she decided, and knocked frantically on Bill's bedroom door.

Kay and her mother stepped softly into his room keeping their voices low so as not to disturb Miss Janey.

"Bill, I'm terribly upset!" Mrs. Tracey whispered. "Someone just phoned to say we'd be sorry if we interfered in any way with the theft of Alice's suitcase."

It took Bill a few seconds to understand fully what was being said. Then he announced cheerfully, "Oh, it's probably just a joke. Don't worry about it. Perhaps some friend of Kay's thought it was a great gag! I'm sure there are a couple of school girls giggling over it this minute!"

"It was a man's voice, Bill."

"Well, it's one of the high school boys, then, teasing Kay because she is always getting involved in mysteries!" Bill assured her.

"I know!" Kay burst out. "It might be Chris Eaton's idea. It'd be just like her to do something like this."

She then told of the girls' encounter with Chris that afternoon and the accident.

"You've hit it, Kay," Bill agreed. "That's exactly it. Chris is playing a practical joke."

Mrs. Tracey gave a sigh of relief. "Yes, that's very likely," she admitted. "The voice did sound as if it were disguised."

Accepting this explanation everyone went back to bed again, their minds at rest in regard to the call.

The next day nothing was said about the phone call to Miss Janey. The phone had not awakened her and she was so refreshed by her sound sleep that she insisted upon moving into her new home.

"I am not going to stay here and impose on you, Kathryn," she said. "Besides, I am eager to get settled in my own place. Then I hope we shall see lots of each other and renew old times!"

Mrs. Tracey and Kay, therefore, devoted the day to helping Miss Janey get settled in the pretty house she had bought on the outskirts of town. It stood on a wooded hill overlooking the river. The view was beautiful but Kay was thinking that the place was a little too lonely. At twilight Miss Janey herself noticed this feature.

"Dear me," she said with a shiver, "I shall have to get a housekeeper companion here. I don't think I want to live alone this far from town and so near those woods! In fact," she added, "I rather dread spending this first night by myself. I don't suppose, Kay, that you could stay with me? Tomorrow I'll look for a housekeeper."

"I'll be glad to stay!" said Kay although she had a feeling that the blonde thief or his female partner might pay an unwelcome visit.

Perhaps this idea kept her from sleeping soundly that night. At any rate, Kay woke up a number of times to strange sounds.

"Is that my imagination, or do I really hear voices?" she wondered finally.

It was two in the morning, yet she was sure she heard voices downstairs. Without turning on a light, Kay crept quietly down the hall.

Someone was down there alright. The light was on in the kitchen.

Kay leaned cautiously over the banister and peered through the kitchen door. The sight that met her eyes was stranger than anything she could have imagined.

Miss Janey, in her bathrobe, was staring at a strange old woman who looked like a witch.

"Another Woman of Mystery!" marveled Kay.

IV

The Witch's Prophecy

Miss Janey seemed to be completely under the power of this woman. Speaking in hushed tones and making slow motions with her hands as she did so the wrinkled old woman seemed to have hypnotized Miss Janey.

"This meeting is so strange," Kay thought. "Miss Janey is definitely keeping something from us. There must be more to this robbery than she wants to tell."

Kay listened intently and finally was able to make out what the crone was saying:

"You see a lonely wood. A deep, gloomy wood. And now you see a house in those woods. It is dark and empty. Hear its shutters rattling in the wind! Now see a woman moving through the trees toward that house, in the black night. She enters! She opens a dusty cupboard door and there——

"—there lies a suitcase and a purse!" she cackled, weaving her hands to and fro before Miss Janey's face. "Yes, there they are, still filled with your treasures, untouched. Follow the trail to the lonely house in the wood, by night, and recover them before approaching dark figures wrest your fortune from you!"

The old woman let her hands fall suddenly and the spell seemed to be broken. Miss Janey sighed, moved and spoke.

"Thank you so much. You are always such a help. I'll do as you say," she said, pressing some bills into the outstretched palm.

Mumbling over the money, the old woman shuffled out and vanished into the snowy night.

"Probably flew off on a broomstick!" Kay thought with a nervous chuckle.

Then she crouched out of sight as Miss Janey, moving like a sleepwalker, ascended the staircase and passed her.

"She actually consulted a medium about her stolen things," Kay reasoned. "And it sounds like she's known that woman for some time.

"Maybe Miss Janey moved to Brantwood to be near this strange woman. I can't wait to see if those directions will actually lead her to her things. If they do, I bet that old fraud hid them there herself. I wouldn't be surprised if that awful old woman were in cahoots with the thieves."

Kay was so keyed up that she thought she would never get to sleep. She did, however, and slept so soundly that she did not wake up until the sun was shining in her eyes and Miss Janey's footsteps were echoing from the kitchen. The woman was calmly preparing breakfast as if nothing strange had happened during the night.

In fact Kay found herself wondering whether she had not dreamed the whole thing. She was relieved when the twins showed up to ask her to go skiing with them.

"That was great!" Kay exclaimed later, when a morning of skiing had blown the cobwebs from her confused brain. "I even forgot about the theft." She laughed, "But here we are back at the house and we've got to get to work solving this case."

"What a gorgeous car! Whose is it?" Wendy asked, pausing to admire a car in the driveway.

"That must be Miss Janey's new car. Isn't it a beauty!" Kay said.

The girls' inspection of it was interrupted by the arrival of a brisk young woman asking, "Does a Miss Alice Janey live here? She phoned in answer to my newspaper ad for a position as a maid. I've come for an interview. My name is Jessie Hipple."

The applicant seemed to be very competent and quite pleasant. Both Kay and Miss Janey were satisfied with her so the girl was hired.

Kay and her friends were about to go home when two burly policemen arrived at the house.

"Do you have any news for me?" Miss Janey asked.

"We haven't caught your thief yet, Ma'am," replied one of the men.

"But we are following several clues and expect to recover your property before long," the other assured her.

The officers then began questioning her on specific points of the case. Kay was worried that this might scare off the new maid but the girl seemed so interested and sympathetic that Kay's fears were dispelled.

Kay was astonished to hear Miss Janey suddenly

remark, "I feel perfectly confident of regaining my belongings, for I dreamed that they are hidden in a certain empty house. I have great faith in dreams."

Kay took the twins aside and quickly briefed them on the strange meeting with the old woman.

"She didn't dream it, or if she did, I had the same dream!" Kay explained. "I certainly saw that weird old witch and heard her tell where Miss Janey's things are hidden!"

"Let's follow Miss Janey when she goes to that house tonight!" Betty said eagerly.

At Miss Janey's urging, the girls stayed for the rest of the day. It was a very long day, the girls thought, but at last the sun set. Sure enough, at dusk Miss Janey set off in her new car.

Kay and her friends promptly followed. By the time they reached "the deep, gloomy wood" it was quite dark and only the glimmer of the taillight ahead served to guide them over the lonely country road.

"Hurry, Kay, we may lose her!" Betty said as the light vanished abruptly. "She must have turned into that lane."

The engine groaned and the wheels of the car skidded and whirred in the struggle through the deep snow. Ahead, through the trees, was an old house. Miss Janey paused before it a moment, then got out of the car.

"It's all just like the woman said!" Kay said. "And there goes Miss Janey, making her way through the dark to the house just as she was told to do."

"Let's park here. We'll make better time on foot!" suggested Betty.

The three girls got out of the car and plunged through the drifts. They could barely make out Miss Janey stumbling up the slippery path to the dismal house. As the gleam of her flashlight played over the porch, they saw a great door suddenly yawn open and close on her. For a moment the woman's flashlight blinked and flitted through the windows like a restless lightning-bug, then it was extinguished and it was totally dark.

The girls forged on through the deep snow. Kay, quicker than the others, hustled ahead. Wendy trying to catch up, lunged forward and suddenly felt the ground give way beneath her feet. She shot dizzily through space in a breathless landslide. Down, down she coasted, loose snow piling over her head as she sank into an unseen pit.

Betty, just behind, clutched wildly at her sister and tried to drag her back. Her added weight sent more snow cascading into the hole and whirled her down on top of Wendy. Both were smothered under a cave-in of more snow sliding upon them from above.

Buried under the avalanche, the twins beat madly upward toward the surface, fighting for air.

Their muffled cries for help stopped Kay dead in her tracks.

V

Double Trouble

"Where are you?" Kay shouted as she ran in the direction of the twins' frantic screams.

"H-e-r-e! H-e-l-p!"

Kay looked around wildly. There was no sign of the girls, yet they were calling from close by.

"W-h-e-r-e?" she yelled.

"H-e-r-e!"

The cries grew sharper but the twins remained invisible.

Suddenly, there was an upheaval of the ground. Kay's mouth fell open with amazement as she beheld two ghosts rise out of the earth at her feet. A moment later, the ghosts had off their white veils of snow and revealed themselves as two very wet and shaken ghost girls!

"What in the world—?" Kay gasped.

"We fell into a hole!" Betty explained.

"Careful, Kay, or you'll fall in it too!" Wendy warned, as her friend stepped near it.

"This whole thing gives me the creeps." Betty shivered. "First a mysterious midnight rendezvous, then our finding this house in the woods exactly like the medium said——"

"And you two vanishing and returning from the inside of the earth!" Kay finished. "Come on, hurry. We've got to see if Miss Janey finds her things in the cupboard!"

But their mishap had quenched the twins' thirst for adventure.

"You couldn't pay me to go into that haunted house!" Betty declared flatly.

"I don't want to, either," Wendy wailed. "Don't go, Kay!" she pleaded. "Please."

"I most certainly am going," Kay said. "I wouldn't miss it for anything! You can wait here if you want to," she added and ran off.

"Oh, dear," Wendy moaned, "if anything happens to Kay I'd be afraid to go into that spooky place after her!"

"I hope she'll be alright!" said Betty as she and her sister jumped and stamped their feet vigorously to warm up.

Meanwhile, Kay had reached the dark porch and was fumbling for the doorknob. It turned easily and the huge door swung open, revealing a dark and empty hall. She listened intently for some sound of Miss Janey, but the place was absolutely quiet.

Suddenly the crunch of footsteps on the snow outside broke the stillness. When Kay heard the heavy tread of feet on the porch she shrank into a shadowy corner.

Realizing it was probably the police, following up Miss Janey's story of her dream, Kay was just about to step out when a flashlight at the door revealed two men. She could see them plainly; they were not the police.

Coat collars up, and hats pulled down over their faces, the two men slipped inside. Kay flattened herself against the wall. Finding a coat closet behind her, she slipped inside.

Just in time! The men would have certainly spotted her, had she not slowly pulled the closet door shut. She could hear them going from room to room.

"Hey, what's that?" one of them called out.

"Where?" echoed the answer.

"There, on the floor!"

There was a moment of silence, then a long-drawn-out whistle of surprise. Kay cautiously peeked out of a crack.

"Why, it's a woman!" both men cried out together.

Kay trembled with fear. What could have happened to Miss Janey?

"Dead, do you suppose?" asked one man.

There was a shuffle of feet, then silence and finally, "No, she's not dead. What'll we do with her?"

"Carry her down the trail."

Again a shuffle of feet along the hall and the bang of the front door followed by a crunching of footsteps on the snow.

Kay waited a moment, then ventured from her hiding place to the porch. She could make out the footprints but the men themselves were out of sight. And with them Miss Janey!

From the opposite direction to that taken by the men, Betty and Wendy were plowing through the snow.

"Are you all right?" Wendy called.

"Did you see those men?" Betty asked.

"What were they carrying?" Wendy inquired.

"I think they had Miss Janey!" Kay told them excitedly.

"W-h-a-t!" exploded the twins.

"Quick, let's follow them. If they do have Miss Janey, we've got to rescue her!"

The girls ran off in the direction the men had gone. They didn't get far however, because the wind seemed to have blown loose snow over the footprints. With no tracks to follow, the girls turned back.

"Perhaps it wasn't Miss Janey after all. Maybe she is still in the house though I doubt it," reflected Kay.

Back at the house, the girls looked for Miss Janey but there was no sign of her nor of anyone else.

"I thought this house was supposed to be empty," Wendy said.

"It is empty," Betty replied.

"But it's full of furniture. It looks like someone lives here."

"I don't think anyone does," Betty said.

Her words were interrupted by a loud crash.

"What was that?" Wendy asked.

"Ouch! I hit my head on an open cupboard door!" Kay moaned. "Why, what—?"

"What is it, Kay?" Betty asked.

"What is it and where are you? I can't see a thing," Wendy complained.

"I'm here. I grabbed at that cupboard to keep my balance and look——"

"How can we? It's too dark," Betty answered irritably.

"Do your best," Kay encouraged. "Guess what I've found?"

"What!" the twins asked impatiently.

"I'VE FOUND MISS JANEY'S BAGS!"

"What!" the twins squealed.

Betty and Wendy squatted down on the floor near Kay and squinted at the discovery.

"It's incredible!" said Betty.

"That witch-like woman was right," Wendy said. "How did you——"

"When I grabbed at the cupboard," Kay explained, "my hand touched a panel that slid back and out fell these bags!"

"A secret compartment!" Wendy exclaimed, examining the cabinet.

"It's the 'dusty cupboard,' the medium described!" stated Kay. "Now let's see if the rest of the prophecy comes true and the valuables are still here."

With the twins crowded close to look Kay opened the suitcase and the purse but they were both completely empty.

"That's the first time the prophecy has failed," Betty said.

"No," Kay answered slowly. "The prophecy hasn't failed; in fact, it's been pretty accurate. As I recall Miss Janey was warned to hurry and reclaim her things before two dark figures, would 'wrest her fortune from her.' Well, those men who were here were plainly the two dark figures. They seem to have made off with not only the fortune, but Miss Janey herself."

The three friends stood in the dark, mysterious house, too disappointed to say anything more for a few moments. Suddenly the silence was broken by a soft swish of movement. The next moment a voice croaked:

"Begone! Begone at once!"

Wendy and Betty caught Kay by her wrists and fled, dragging their friend with them in a frenzy of fear. As they ran laughter rang out after them, followed by the slamming of the massive front door.

VI

Chris's Triumph

"Stop!" Kay pleaded. "We've got to go back! I think I recognized that voice!"

It was useless for her to plead or struggle, the twins kept running, hauling Kay along between them.

"We're getting out of here and you're coming with us!" Wendy urged.

At last the girls reached their car and they scrambled inside and took off.

"We'll stop off and see if Miss Janey is at home or missing," Kay said.

Jessie Hipple, the new maid, greeted the girls with a very worried expression.

"Is Miss Janey with you?" she asked.

"No, we were hoping she'd be here," Kay replied.

"I wonder what could have happened. She's awfully late." Jessie nervously said.

"This looks serious!" Kay whispered to the twins.

"I've had supper ready and waiting for hours and now it's all spoiled!" complained the maid.

"I'm sure Miss Janey will be back any minute now," Kay said to calm Jessie down.

"We'd better be going," put in Wendy.

"Oh, do you have to? I wish you would stay," Jessie pleaded. "I hate to be left here all by myself. I'm so worried."

"I don't blame you," sympathized Wendy.

"We'd stay," Betty assured her, "but our families are expecting us."

"I'd better go home for a while at least," said Kay thoughtfully. "If Miss Janey doesn't come back soon, Jessie, let me know and I'll come right over."

"I'm anxious to talk to Bill about all this," said Kay when the girls were back in the car.

"It's mysterious alright," Betty said.

"It looks like a kidnaping." Kay sighed. "We may need a lawyer and a lot of help to rescue Miss Janey."

When Kay got home she found her mother alone in the study, knitting.

"Where's Bill?" was the first thing she said as she burst into the room.

"He had an appointment and didn't come home for supper," her mother replied.

Mrs. Tracey was so engrossed in her knitting that she didn't notice Kay's excitement. Kay took her off guard with the alarming news of Miss Janey's disappearance.

"If I only knew where to get in touch with Bill!" Mrs. Tracey moaned. "Maybe we ought to go back to her house soon. From there we can phone around the neighborhood to try to find Bill," Kay suggested.

"Yes, that's a good idea."

"May I have something to eat before we go?" asked Kay.

"Gracious, haven't you had your supper?" Mrs.

Tracey asked and hastily set out odds and ends from the refrigerator.

Kay ate a quick meal, then she and her mother started out for Miss Janey's. Jessie Hipple hurried to let them in and asked them to keep their voices down.

"Miss Janey's back," the maid whispered, "but she's gone to bed with a splitting headache. She said she didn't want to be disturbed under any circumstances."

"Did she say anything about where she had been or what delayed her?" Kay asked.

"No, not a word," Jessie answered. "She just went to her room. I'm sure she'll be alright in the morning."

"Well," said Mrs. Tracey, "if we can be of any help, don't hesitate to call. Take good care of her, Jessie. She's an old and dear friend of mine."

"I'll take care of her," the maid promised.

"What a relief," Kay said as she and her mother left. "We were scared to death about her being kidnaped and here she is, safe and sound in bed. Don't you think we ought to celebrate?"

"By all means," her mother laughed. "Let's go to the movies."

Mother and daughter went off to the movies in high spirits. They settled down when all of a sudden it sputtered and stopped. At the same moment loud, angry voices could be heard coming from the film.

Someone shouted "Come with us!" and in response there was a furious, "Get outa here!" Then a deep voice roared, "You're under arrest!"

The audience, confused and afraid was in an uproar.

"Stop, thief!" someone cried.

"Catch him!"

"It's the police!"

Somebody screamed, "Don't shoot!" This was

followed by hysterical shrieks and wild confusion as the audience tried to get out. A woman near Kay was knocked down and trampled. Another fainted. Some policemen had arrived on the scene and were trying to quiet the crowd.

Kay was pulling her mother, who had lost her coat, to a side exit, when she heard a familiar voice.

"Why, it's Chris Eaton," said Kay.

"What's she saying?" Mrs. Tracey asked crossly.

Chris answered this herself by proclaiming loudly to the crowd, "I'm the one who recognized that thief. I saw him through the booth window there. I knew he was the man they've all been looking for. He stole a lady's purse and suitcase at the station the other day. I knew him the minute I laid eyes on him. I never forget a face." Chris continued. "I slipped out quietly and got the police to come and arrest him. To think he was in here operating the film all the time they were looking for him."

The thief who was now firmly in the hands of two policemen in the lobby suddenly clutched his mouth and stomach and mumbled, "I'm sick."

He bolted into the wash room, while Chris continued boasting about her cleverness at securing his arrest.

"That'll be a feather in your cap, young lady!" the policeman on guard at the washroom door said.

Another officer pushed past him, club in hand, and followed the thief. One glance at the room and the man stormed out shouting:

"He got away! The washroom's empty and the window's open!"

VII

A Bold Demand

Chris Eaton was quite flattered by the compliment the policeman had paid her. She found herself day-dreaming in school, imagining interviews with reporters who wanted her picture and story for the newspapers.

"My picture? No, please!" was one of her imaginary conversations. "After all, what have I done? Only my duty as a citizen. It was nothing. Well, if you insist. But I don't know why you would want to feature a picture of me!"

But it didn't happen that way. No one took any notice of her achievement. No reporters sought her out.

Being ignored infuriated her.

"Miss Janey owes me something for identifying the movie operator as the thief."

One afternoon, unable to stand it any longer, she went to Miss Janey's to demand a reward. It provoked her to find Kay there.

Kay and Miss Janey had become good friends and Kay often dropped in for a visit. Neither of them was overjoyed when Jessie Hipple ushered in Chris Eaton.

"I wonder, Miss Janey, if you realize I was the one who identified your robber?" she began.

"Why yes, I believe I owe you a debt of gratitude," the woman responded.

"Don't you think you owe me something more than gratitude?" Chris said.

Kay flushed angrily but Miss Janey answered graciously, "Possibly I do. I had thought of offering a reward for the apprehension of the criminal and the return of my valuables."

"But the thief escaped and your belongings are still missing!" Kay cut in, astounded at Chris's boldness.

"You keep out of this, Kay! It's none of your business."

"Well I'm certainly not going to let you talk to my mother's friend this way!"

"Oh, I suppose you want to be the one to get the reward by catching the man yourself!" the unpleasant girl sneered.

Miss Janey was distressed. "I do want to compliment you, Chris, on your cleverness in identifying the man. Who knows but you may succeed later in having him captured? If you do, you can be sure I'll give you a generous reward."

So saying, the woman smiled and rose in courteous dismissal, while Jessie Hipple briskly showed Chris to the door.

Chris spread a story at school that her brilliance as a sleuth went unrewarded "because of the stinginess of the old maid." Chris only succeeded in being ridiculed. The school paper printed a cartoon of her marked, FOILED AGAIN! The picture showed a likeness of Chris holding a magnifying glass in one hand and a butterfly net in the other. Escaping from the net was a butterfly labelled THIEF.

But none of this discouraged Chris. She was as interested as ever in sleuthing. She began devouring detective stories and for English class wrote a short paper entitled "Great Detectives."

She was so proud of her story that she gave it to one of the boys to read just before the period when the work was to be handed in. He in turn passed it around to several students.

Chris was delighted to be called to read her paper aloud to the class. Stepping to the front of the room she began to read quite energetically. Suddenly she stopped.

"Go on," the teacher, Miss Waters, encouraged.

Stammering Chris read a little further, then stopped again.

"Come, come, Miss Eaton, can't you read your own handwriting?"

Embarrassed, Chris murmured something under her breath and went to her seat.

"Miss Eaton, you must hand in your paper," Miss Waters said firmly.

"Please I'd rather not," the girl pleaded.

"Bring it to my desk at once!" the teacher insisted.

Reluctantly Chris laid her paper on Miss Waters's desk and returned to her seat.

"Now let us see what is in this paper," the teacher remarked.

Chris's composition, as she had written it, went something like this:

GREAT DETECTIVES

Did you know that the Prophet Daniel who once was thrown to the lions, became a great detective? He tried to convince the king that the huge heathen idol did not really eat the banquet spread before it. One night Daniel strewed ashes on the floor around this idol. The next day he showed the king the telltale footprints of people who came to steal the food by night. This is an early record of detecting by tracing footprints.

Other solutions have been employed. In the story of *The Gold Bug* the hero shows how to decipher a puzzling code. The policeman who pursued *Jean Valjean*, the escaped convict, shows the value of persistence in following a trail no matter how cold. *Sherlock Holmes* made famous the principle of "deduction" in solving crime, which is used today by our G-Men.

It is my hope to become a great detective myself some day, perhaps the first woman to gain fame in this field!

This was Chris's original wording, but not what Miss Waters read. She saw her own name on the page, as well as mention of Miss Conway, the history teacher, Mr. Reynolds, the dramatic coach, Miss Hanson, the gym teacher, even the high school principal. She read aloud from the paper as follows:

"Did you know that Miss Waters, who once was thrown to the lions, became a great detective? She tried to convince Miss Conway that the heathen Mr. Reynolds did not eat the banquet set before him."

An explosion of laughter shook the class. Miss Waters rapped for order and tried to go on, but the account of Miss Hanson, the gym teacher pursuing the escaped convict, the high school principal, threw the students into shrieks.

Finally Miss Waters pounded for order and asked, "What is the meaning of this, Miss Eaton?"

Springing to her feet Chris cried out, "I didn't write it that way, Miss Waters! Someone has changed the names to get me in trouble! I think someone showed it to Kay Tracey and she did it!"

The students all came to Kay's defense and Miss Waters announced that the matter would be taken up after class.

"It was so funny I didn't even mind being blamed for it," Kay said to the twins as she set out after school to visit Miss Janey.

Kay saw Miss Janey fairly often, partly because of a real liking for her, and partly from her desire to get to the bottom of the robbery and Miss Janey's strange meeting with the medium.

Kay had promptly returned to Miss Janey the empty purse and suitcase she had found in the "haunted house." Up to this time, however, no mention had been made by either of them of the old witch-like woman.

"It was strange that you went to that particular house to look for your things," Kay said. "You say you saw it in a dream?"

"Not exactly," confessed Miss Janey. "It was clairvoyance. The scene was revealed to me by an old woman who has mystic powers."

"You don't really believe that kind of thing, do you?" Kay asked.

"'Nanna,' has been advising me for a long time now and has proved herself reliable. What she says comes true."

Miss Janey spoke so sharply that Kay decided it would be best to make no further comment.

Miss Janey avoided further reference to the adventure at the house in the woods and did not divulge what had happened to her the night the men carried her away. Kay, of course was dying to know, but not wanting to pry she changed the subject.

"Do you have any plans for this winter?" she asked, recalling some reference to work Miss Janey hoped to complete.

"Yes, I'm going to be working on some chemical research," the woman announced enthusiastically. "My dear father was a chemist and inventor. We used to work long hours together in his laboratory. His many patents still yield me a good income from royalties.

"It was his secret formula for a new substance, similar to glass but having more uses, which was in my safe deposit box. This is more valuable, really, than anything else I have. Now that this formula has been stolen, I am afraid my father's work may be lost or sold by the thief."

"You don't have a copy of it?" Kay asked.

"Unfortunately no. There is one hope, however. My father had not perfected certain points but no one knew this but myself. My plan is to complete this work in his memory. I have had one of the rooms here fitted up as a laboratory. Would you like to see it?"

"I'd love to," Kay said eagerly. "Chemistry has always been one of my favorite subjects. How exciting, to have a laboratory of your own!"

While Miss Janey was showing Kay the laboratory Jessie interrupted to say that "Nanna" was at the door. Miss Janey urged Kay to try her hand at some simple experiments, and left to greet Nanna. Alone in the laboratory, Kay was soon at work on one of her high school chemistry problems. After a few minutes she paused, test tube in hand. She had an uncomfortable feeling that someone was watching.

Glancing over her shoulder she was startled to see a sinister face peering through a window at some important papers on Miss Janey's desk. Reacting quickly Kay decided to turn out the light. She reached out and pulled a switch.

An explosion knocked Kay to the floor and a small fire started spreading toward Miss Janey's papers. Kay, in a helpless heap on the floor, watched it, but she was unable to move a finger.

VIII

An Unexpected Announcement

"Fire! Fire!" Jessie shrieked as she raced toward the laboratory. With a frantic screech for help the maid pounced on Kay and dragged her out of harm's way.

Feeling now returned to Kay's hands and feet and she quickly joined Jessie in beating out the fire, snatching Miss Janey's papers away just in time.

All the commotion finally stirred Miss Janey who had been in another part of the house. To Kay's amazement she seemed remarkably calm as she helped put out the blaze.

"It was all my fault," said Kay. "I'm terribly sorry."

"How did it happen?" asked Jessie.

Kay explained about the face at the window, the seemingly important papers and her attempt to protect them by turning off the lights.

"You simply pulled the wrong switch," explained Miss Janey, unconcernedly. "I knew this fire was going to occur. It's not your fault, my dear, but just part of Fate's pattern! I had already been warned of it. Old

Nanna came to the door to tell me about a fire which would threaten my property. No sooner had the words left her mouth than I heard Jessie scream.

"Perhaps you now see why I have so much faith in Nanna. I'm thankful to you for rescuing my papers. They are quite important. You have helped me wonderfully and you are not to worry about your part of the accident. I am sure a fire would have broken out, even if you had not been here."

"I'll bet the old witch or an accomplice was peering through the window, and saw the whole thing," Kay reflected. "Maybe they even planned to steal those papers and then set fire to the place. My being here and causing a fire probably was just a coincidence."

Kay hurried home to consult with Bill.

When Kay got home she found Bill in the living room with two men. As Kay went by, she was struck by something vaguely familiar about the callers.

"Where have I seen them before?" she asked herself.

At that moment Bill noticed her at the doorway and asked her in. He introduced his visitors as Mr. Tilden and Mr. Lee. As soon as the men rose and greeted her Kay remembered where she'd seen them.

"Why, they're the two men who carried Miss Janey away that night!" she thought.

"Kay, these men are detectives and they're helping us with Miss Janey's case," he explained.

That was the last thing she had expected. Yet she was tremendously relieved.

"What did you do with Miss Janey that night you carried her out of the house and into the woods?" she quickly demanded.

The men glanced at each other in surprise, then Mr. Lee asked, "How did you know about that?"

"I was watching through a crack in a closet door!" Kay confessed, laughing at the amazed expressions on their faces.

"Well," said Mr. Tilden to Bill, "you told us Kay was a pretty good detective, but we had no idea she was as hot on the trail as all that!"

"Sounds as if you beat us to it!" chuckled Mr. Lee.

"Well I did find the lost bags—" Kay began.

"You did!" both men interrupted. "Where?"

"They fell out of a secret compartment when I touched a sliding panel by accident," Kay informed them. "But they were empty. By the way, you haven't told me yet just what you did with Miss Janey," said Kay.

"We found her in a dead faint, carried her into the fresh air and revived her. Then we took her home," said Mr. Lee.

Kay learned from the two detectives that Miss Janey was suspected of helping certain persons swindle widows who had been left money. These people promised to double the woman's money but the victims never saw their funds again and often were left penniless. It was to round up this ring that the detectives had been brought into the picture.

"How could anyone suspect Miss Janey of being dishonest!" Kay cried indignantly.

The men were unsympathetic. "Yes, she seems quite respectable, and she's likely to inspire trust. But that's just the thing that would allow her to cheat defenseless widows so easily."

"I can't believe Miss Janey would ever cheat anyone. If she is involved in this scheme I'm sure she is innocent of any wrongdoing. Perhaps she is being used by someone. It is more likely that she herself is being robbed."

"How do you account for her knowing about the house in the woods?" Mr. Tilden asked.

Kay told them about the woman known as Nanna.

"Do you think you could locate this woman?" Mr. Lee asked eagerly.

"Yes, I think so. I don't know where she lives but Miss Janey seems to be in constant touch with her."

"I think we've made real progress in unraveling this mystery," said Mr. Tilden getting up to leave. "If you find that woman call us immediately. In the meantime we'll follow up a few other clues."

Hardly had the door shut then there came a timid knock. Going to open it, Bill explained to Kay who it probably was.

"A rather poverty-stricken client of mine," he whispered. "One of the 'poor widows.'"

The middle-aged woman who entered certainly looked like she'd fallen on hard times. Her black outfit was somewhat shabby, her hat droopy and her face discouraged and unnaturally pale.

"It was all the money I had in the world," she was telling Bill, "and how I was so foolish to risk it I can't understand. I guess I was just so worried about not having enough money to support my children that I was willing to try anything. A man told me I could double my money if I would take it to a certain old house in the woods and I went along with it."

Kay and Bill Tracey exchanged significant glances at this.

"I had almost reached the house," the woman went on, "when I took a wrong turn and lost my way. I asked a stranger to direct me. He very kindly took my arm and helped me through the snow. I was grateful to him at the time but afterwards I discovered my wallet was gone. I am sure that man took it."

"Was there much money in it?" asked Bill.

"Every cent I had in the world! I had drawn it out of the bank to take to that house. Of course I couldn't swear in court that the man stole my money, yet I feel that it was all a plan of his and the person who had come to my house to rob me and perhaps others."

Having related her sad story, the poor widow gave way to tears.

"There, there, Mrs. Dale," encouraged the lawyer. "Things look black now but we are well on the way to solving this case. Keep up your courage and leave things in my hands. I expect to have good news for you within the next few days."

"Kay, will you take me to this mysterious house in the woods?" Bill asked after Mrs. Dale had left.

"I'd be glad to," the girl replied energetically.

Kay and Bill started out at once. When their car turned into the lane that led to the mansion, the snow was still so deep that it seemed best to park and walk the rest of the way. It was a long, cold walk through the snow. The short winter afternoon was nearing an end and already the sunset had dwindled to ash grey.

When they reached the dilapidated porch they pushed open the door and peered in. There was not a sound.

Suddenly, a series of heartrending groans rose through the silence. Kay felt her skin tingle. It sounded like someone was in agony.

IX

"Help!"

For a moment both Kay and Bill froze listening in amazement as the wails echoed through the high-ceilinged room. Finally, after one cry had risen to a high-pitched scream, then died away into a whimper, the listeners stirred.

A thorough search revealed nobody in any of the rooms, but the melancholy cries continued. Sometimes it seemed to come from below, sometimes from an adjoining room.

"It's almost as if someone were shut up inside the wall," Bill reflected.

This gave Kay an idea. After a few minutes of tapping, each tap answered by a wail, she cried out. There at her feet, cleverly concealed, was a trapdoor. Bill wrenched it open on its rusty hinges and the two gazed down into the black depths below. Not a sound! Then came again the pitiful cry. Someone below stirred.

Bill lowered himself into the opening and stooped to find a boy who seemed to be about twelve years old.

"Le'me out! Le'me out!" he cried, nearly wild with fright.

"We'll get you out," Bill said gently lifting the boy out through the trapdoor. "How did you get in there?"

"None o' yer business!" the terrified boy shrieked, scrambling to his feet.

Without another word, the boy raced to the front door, pulled it open, and ran out into the snow.

Kay followed the boy as he bounded over the snow like a rabbit. She was having trouble catching up when suddenly the boy stumbled and sprawled head over heels into a drift.

While he was struggling to get up Kay pounced on him. The boy thrashed about furiously but Kay managed to keep a pretty firm grip on him.

"Good for you, Kay," Bill said when he had caught up. "Let's take him home and see what he can tell us."

By now the boy had stopped struggling and Bill and Kay were easily able to lead him to the car.

"I was trying to get back my mother's money!" the boy suddenly blurted out, breaking into tears.

"Who is your mother, and how did she lose her money?" Bill urged.

"She's Mrs. Dale and I'm Teddy Dale. She came to this house to give her money to some people and they were going to give her twice as much back again. But they never did! They stole it all!"

With that the boy burst into a fresh torrent of tears.

"And—and—I tried to find it and I fell through that hole. Somebody slammed the door shut on top of me and I couldn't get out," he stammered talking through his tears.

Kay mopped his face with her handkerchief and tried to calm him down.

Teddy had quieted down by the time they reached

the Tracey home. Kay warmed up some dinner for him and watched as he gulped down the food.

"He's half starved," Kay thought, "I don't think he gets enough to eat."

At that moment Kay resolved to do all she could to help catch the crooks who were robbing widows and causing children to go hungry!

"If the same swindlers are robbing Miss Janey and the Dales, that gives me two good reasons for catching them," she decided.

Kay drove Teddy home and left him and his mother with the assurance that she, Bill and the detectives would be doing everything they could to help. The very next afternoon Kay was on the case. She was walking along the main street of Brantwood when she bumped into Wendy.

"Hi, Kay! Come and have a soda with me while I wait for Betty to finish at the dentist's."

"I'm on my way to do something in connection with the mystery," Kay said and then she rapidly relayed the latest developments. "I think it's very important that we find out who owns that place," she concluded. "How about going to the tax collector's office with me? They ought to be able to tell us."

At the town hall, the tax collector referred to a huge leather-bound volume for the information the girls wanted.

"That place belongs to an old woman by the name of Mrs. Lucy Larrop," he informed the girls.

"Who's she?" Wendy murmured as the girls left the office.

"That's what I have to find out," Kay asserted.

"How?" Wendy asked.

"First of all I'll ask Miss Janey if she knows the owner of that house. She may, after all, she went there."

"But would she tell you?"

"We'll see," Kay replied. The girls went into a shop for a soda, and Kay went to make a quick phone call. She came out of the phone booth laughing.

"Good news?" Wendy asked.

"Amazing news!" Kay answered. "Miss Janey does know the owner of that old house. "It's Nanna, the old witch!"

"What!"

"I nearly dropped the receiver when she told me," Kay laughed.

"Well, what's our next step?" asked Wendy.

"We ought to talk to Bill before we do anything. We don't want to make any move which might confuse things for the detectives."

Betty, who had been at the dentist's appeared just then and the girls at once told her the latest news. They finished their drinks and hurried to Kay's house.

"Look, it's that poor Mrs. Dale, the mother of the boy we found in the old house," Kay whispered to her friends as they walked in the front door.

Mrs. Tracey was talking with the woman in the living room. "Kay, come in," she called. "Mrs. Dale is in trouble again!"

"Oh, dreadful trouble!" the widow sobbed, dabbing her handkerchief to her wet eyes. "The police have arrested my Teddy!"

"What for?" Kay asked in surprise.

"For breaking and entering. It was because he went into that awful old house to look for my money. And now he's been arrested for attempted burglary!"

With these words the woman broke down and wept.

"Please don't cry," said Kay compassionately. "I'm

sure Bill will get him out. After all, he's only a child. And a child can't be held for burglary!"

Kay announced this with such confidence that Mrs. Dale wiped her eyes and looked up hopefully. "Do you really think it will be all right?"

"Of course!" Kay declared. "I'm going to phone Bill and get his advice."

Bill said they should go at once to the police station and he'd meet them there. Gratefully Mrs. Dale clambered into the car with Kay and the twins, who were dropped off at their house on the way to the station.

Entering the police station, Mrs. Dale gave a little cry at the sight of her son. He looked very small and scared, sitting between two huge officers. Bill was conferring with the chief when Kay and Mrs. Dale walked in.

"Is anyone else coming?" Bill inquired.

"Why no," Kay answered, puzzled.

"Nobody has appeared to press this charge against the boy," Bill explained. "Apparently as soon as it was found that the Dales had backing and that I was here to defend him, the case was called off. Teddy is free to go."

"I'm relieved that Teddy's being released," Kay commented, "but it's too bad the person who complained didn't show up. They might have provided some valuable clues.

"Speaking of clues, you'll never guess who owns that house! The old crone who is Miss Janey's fortune teller, Mrs. Lucy Larrop."

"Very interesting. Still, she may not be living there herself nor does she necessarily have any connection with the present tenants."

"True," agreed Kay. "But I'm convinced she's mixed up in it somehow."

Continuing the discussion, Bill and Kay left the station house. So earnestly were they talking, in fact, that neither one noticed Chris Eaton cross their path and eye them sharply.

After chemistry class the following morning Chris lingered to speak to the head of the department, Doctor Staunton. As Chris laid her notebook on his desk she remarked, "I suppose my work is not as good as Kay Tracey's!"

The teacher replied, "It is not necessary to compare them."

"Perhaps not," Chris answered, "but everybody thinks Kay's so smart."

"She does very good work."

"And no wonder!" Chris retorted. "She gets a lot of help from Miss Alice Janey, the research chemist."

"A splendid opportunity for a student to learn the subject," the instructor remarked.

His delight at Kay's enterprise roused Chris's jealousy still further.

"A splendid opportunity for something else, too," she said with a sly smile. "Perhaps you don't know that Miss Janey is developing her father's famous secret formula and that Kay has stolen it!"

"What are you saying?"

Chris squirmed a little under his piercing glare, but retorted pertly, "Oh, yes, it's well known. Everyone thinks Kay is so perfect but I can tell you this—she has been charged with the theft of the Janey formula!

"Her cousin, who is a lawyer, is trying to defend her. It must be a great disgrace to the family. I saw them coming out of the police station yesterday and Kay was so ashamed she wouldn't speak to me. She kept talking to her cousin and pretending not to see me. I guess after this people will think she's just a little too smart!"

"Are you sure of what you're saying?" asked the teacher.

X

A Problem

Chris was enjoying herself immensely. "Everyone knows that Kay set fire to Miss Janey's laboratory on purpose to make it look like the important papers had been burned. Instead she pocketed them but she was caught."

With these words the troublemaker flounced out of the room to spread the scandal throughout the school. By noon she had managed to convince herself it was true. However, the story had not yet reached Kay and she was therefore surprised to be handed an envelope by Ronald Earle with a summons in it.

"I was asked to give this to you."

Kay glanced at the note as the two strolled down the corridor together.

CARMONT HIGH SCHOOL
OFFICE OF THE PRINCIPAL

Miss Tracey is to come to this office after school today for an interview with Mr. Preston and Doctor Staunton regarding her chemistry.

"I can't imagine what this is for," she said. "My grades in chemistry have been satisfactory."

"Probably going to give you an award," said Ronald.

When Kay reached the principal's office, she found Doctor Staunton going over her papers and notebook with Mr. Preston. She could not help overhearing the chemistry teacher's comment.

"This student has done excellent work, quite beyond anyone in the class."

Just as Kay felt a little swell of pride, she was astounded to hear Mr. Preston remark, "On the other hand, do you think this is her own work, or has she turned in someone else's?"

Horrified, Kay froze in her tracks. There must be some mistake!

Both men looked up as Kay entered the room. Their expressions were exceptionally stern and the reason was soon made clear to Kay. "Kay, Doctor Staunton has been going over your work with me and we agree that it is remarkably good," Mr. Preston said. "It is so remarkable, in fact, that we are wondering whether it is your own or whether you are passing in papers done by a professional."

Kay flushed scarlet. Never had such an accusation been made to her. For a moment she was speechless. Unfortunately, her silence was interpreted by the men as being an admission of guilt.

"We have reason to think," said the chemistry teacher, "that Miss Alice Janey has been doing your work for you."

Kay was furious now.

"That is completely untrue. I would never dream of doing such a thing! Miss Janey has taught me in her private laboratory but that's all. How can you even suspect someone like her of doing anything at all dishonest!"

"She may not realize what you're doing," Mr. Preston suggested. "Let me ask you a question: Is it true that you have stolen her father's formula and been taken to the police about it?"

"I have never stolen anything in my life," Kay replied with a look of utter astonishment. "I don't know what's going on here but I'm determined to find out."

Kay stomped out of the room without another word.

"What was it all about?" asked Ronald, who had been waiting for her in the hall.

When she had told him, Ronald gave a long, indignant whistle.

"I just don't understand. Why on earth would Mr. Preston and Doctor Staunton think I'm a cheat and a thief?"

On the train ride home Kay told Ronald all about Miss Janey and the stolen bags.

"I'll bet Chris Eaton is at the bottom of today's incident. She seemed like she was up to something today. She may have spread the story among the students and gone to the teachers as well. She's jealous of you for many reasons and wants more than anything to ruin your reputation and get attention for herself. She's crazy and those teachers ought to have sense enough to know it!" Ronald growled.

"I'd like to take another look at that house in the woods," Kay said. "I think the answer to many of these problems lies there. Would you come with me? I hate to go alone, and I don't think Mrs. Worth wants Betty and Wendy going out there."

"Of course I'll go. When? How about now?"

"No, I can't go today. I've got to see Miss Janey this

afternoon and ask her to clear up this trouble of mine with the chemistry department. Let's make it tomorrow."

"Tomorrow it is."

Kay went on to Miss Janey's where she found the woman just finishing some laboratory work. The two settled down for a chat in front of the fireplace. Miss Janey was very sympathetic as she listened to Kay's story.

"Don't worry about a thing. I'll talk to those men and explain everything," she promised. "That Doctor Staunton ought to be a reasonable person. I've heard very good things about him. He's written some very interesting papers for the Chemical Society and appears to be most intelligent."

The next day Miss Janey called Doctor Staunton to set up an appointment. Staunton however, wanted to spare Miss Janey the trip to Carmont and insisted on coming out to her home.

The following afternoon Doctor Staunton arrived at Miss Janey's and the two hit it off instantly. Chatting together as if they had been life-long friends they found that they knew many of the same people and had a lot of interests in common. Furthermore Doctor Staunton was an ardent admirer of the work Miss Janey's father had done.

It was some time before either of them thought of Kay and her school work. By then there was no doubt in the teacher's mind that the story about her had been a false one.

"Look, there's Doctor Staunton's car parked in front of your friend's door," said Ronald as he and Kay drove by on their way to the house in the woods.

"It was nice of him to come all the way out here," Kay commented. "By this time I hope he's convinced that I didn't steal the formula."

"Maybe something will turn up at the old house," said Ronald. "If you found the suitcase in that cupboard and if the formula was in the bag when it was stolen, then maybe it is still hidden in another secret compartment. Who knows?"

"The snow is really coming down," Ronald said as he and Kay parked and started floundering ahead in the deep snow.

"I think we're in for a blizzard."

"Who's that?" Ronald asked suddenly, pointing to a hunched figure silhouetted briefly against the driving snow.

"It looks like the old witch Nanna!" Kay cried. "The way she's locking up the place, she must live there.

"Quick, let's ask her some questions!" Kay urged.

They plunged ahead through the storm, but the old woman had vanished.

"How disappointing," said Kay.

"At least we know now that she lives here herself and does not rent the house out," Ronald remarked.

"Let's go in the house," Kay urged. "It's just as well Nanna's out. Now we can look around.

"I'll be glad to get inside!" Kay panted, running up on the porch steps. "Oh, the door is locked!"

"Of course it is. We just saw the old woman lock it. I'll climb to the porch roof and try to open a window."

He swung himself up and Kay saw his boots dangle in mid-air a moment, then vanish.

"It's slippery up here!" she heard him say. "I—oh——"

The loose snow on the roof gave way and it and Ronald went flying into space.

XI

The Disguise

"Are you hurt?" Kay gasped, running to Ronald as he landed in the icy snow.

"I seem to be okay," he said as Kay helped him get up.

Ronald was shaking himself like a wet dog when he suddenly stopped and stood absolutely still.

"What's the matter?" Kay asked, peering back over her shoulder in the direction in which the boy was staring so intently.

"Who's that going into the house?" Ronald whispered.

Two men were entering the house by a side door.

"They must be the swindlers," Kay muttered.

She crouched low and scurried toward the side door. Ronald followed slowly, still a little unsteady from his fall. Entering the house Kay caught a glimpse of the men going upstairs. Both blonde, one was slender, the other thick-set. Kay instantly recognized the slender one.

"It's the man who stole Miss Janey's bags, the one

Chris Eaton identified. I remember hearing the police say his name was Jack Beardsley. I wonder who the other man is?"

The men disappeared upstairs and their footsteps could be heard across the floor above.

From the coat closet which had sheltered her on the former occasion Kay hoped to see and hear as much as possible without being seen.

After a long wait, Kay heard footsteps. What she saw when she peeked out was amazing. Instead of men, two women were coming down the stairs. One was young, slender and blonde. The other made Kay gasp in astonishment.

"That's Nanna! But I just saw her go out! How could she have returned without my seeing her? Or does she have a twin?"

Kay strained to get a better look in the dim hall light which had been turned on. Surely there could be no mistake! There was the old crone, hunched over, shuffling along in her disheveled garments, her arms out, fingers crooked. Then a man's deep voice startled Kay.

"Do I look like the old witch?" and "Nanna" straightened up and laughed.

"You're the image of her!" chuckled the young woman.

Kay noticed that the slender blonde, who was stylishly dressed had unusually large and clumsy feet.

"They're both men dressed as women!" Kay realized. "That slender one makes a pretty good looking girl except for his feet! He can't disguise them. And that bigger man is perfect as Nanna. I wonder what they are up to?"

The men began to talk over their plans and Kay listened intently.

"We'll flag that 7:35 train down there by that lonely

stretch of marshland. There won't be another train along for two and a half hours. That'll give us plenty of time."

"How'll we work it?"

"Easy. Wave the red lights to stop the train and then ask to come aboard explaining that we got lost in the blizzard and your poor, feeble old aunt—that's me—isn't well."

"Then what?"

"After we get aboard we'll hold up the passengers. The train will soon hit that pile of snow we put on the tracks and until somebody clears the rails the train is stuck. That will give us plenty of time for our robbery and escape."

"I hope it works out as easy as it sounds."

"Don't worry. It'll pan out as sure as my name is Ollie Desrale."

"Let's eat before we go," Beardsley suggested. As the two men headed for the kitchen, Kay struggled to think of a way to foil their plan. Noticing that they'd left a knitting bag on the hall table, Kay crept out to examine it.

Feeling inside, Kay pulled out a half-knit sweater, and a ball of wool with needles thrust through it. Underneath lay the men's wallets and watches. Hearing footsteps, Kay quickly set both watches back thirty-five minutes, put them back in the bag and tiptoed out the front door.

"That ought to delay them and perhaps save the train," she thought with a smile.

"Where in the world have you been?" Ronald asked, as Kay emerged onto the porch.

"Sh!" cautioned the girl, and rapidly reported what she'd seen in the house.

"Whew!" the boy whistled in astonishment. "Let's wreck their car so they can't go," he suggested.

"Good idea!" Kay said and the two raced off through the storm to find the thieves' car.

"Here it is." Ronald cried as they came upon the car. "And we're in luck—they left the keys in it."

Ronald started up the engine and drove the car into a ditch.

"It'll take a long time to get that out!" Ronald triumphed as the two started away.

"Look out," Kay warned as she noticed the two "women" making their way toward the car.

Sliding and stumbling Ronald and Kay ran through the snow toward their own car which they found nearly buried in snow.

Loud angry voices, could be heard in the distance. The men were each blaming the other for having left the car to slide into the ditch.

"Let's get out of here," Ronald said, struggling frantically to start the motor.

The engine was so cold it made only a hopeless whirring sound.

"Hurry, here they come!" Kay said.

Drawn by the sounds of the dead engine the two men in disguises now approached rapidly. Speaking in a high voice Beardsley said:

"Our car seems to be stuck in a ditch. I wonder if you would be so kind as to give my aunt and me a lift. We're going to the main road near the railroad track. It's not far."

Without waiting for an answer, the "aunt" got into the back seat. Her "niece" then climbed in too, murmuring, "So kind of you young people."

On the third try Ronald was able to start the car and under cover of the roar of the motor he whispered to Kay, "A chance to drive them straight to the police station."

Ronald drove along as quickly as the storm would

allow, but both he and Kay could tell that the "ladies" in the rear were considerably impatient.

"What time is it, my dear?" the false "Nanna" finally asked.

Kay could hardly keep from laughing as she heard a fumbling in the knitting bag.

"Oh, that can't be right. It's much too slow," the older one said. "The other watch is in there too, isn't it? See what time it says."

"Why, this one must be slow, too! I just know it's later than this!" exclaimed the other.

Ronald hoped the frosted windows would obscure his having taken a turn away from the railroad tracks. Old "Auntie," however, was too alert not to notice.

"You're going the wrong way!" she called out sharply as she cleaned off her window and peered out.

"Turn back, smarty," ordered the other roughly.

Dropping their disguises, they ordered the car stopped and while Desrale yanked Ronald into the back seat, Beardsley climbed into the driver's seat.

As he took the wheel, he got a good look at Kay for the first time. Recognizing her, he immediately started speaking to his companion in a foreign language which neither Kay nor Ronald understood.

They were late and Kay was hoping the train had already passed. Unfortunately the blizzard had made it late and as they headed back toward the tracks they heard the whistle of the approaching train.

"Hurry up!" Desrale prodded.

"How can I hurry in snow like this?" Beardsley growled gritting his teeth.

Suddenly the car skidded wildly finally coming to a stop. Frantically, the two men climbed out of the car and ran off toward the train tracks.

XII

A Train Robbery

Kay just sat there stunned for a few moments as she watched Ronald disappear in the direction the two men had gone. Everything had happened so fast.

Suddenly two signals flashed. The oncoming train answered with a drawn-out whistle and then shuddered to a sudden standstill.

Kay ran toward the train but by the time she reached it the two men had already been allowed to board.

Clearly framed in a bright window, the disguised figures could be seen entering the car.

No one seemed to suspect them!

Kay continued to watch as the pair moved to the front of the car. Suddenly they whipped out revolvers and moments later the passengers flung their arms up high over their heads.

"Start handin' over everything you got!" Beardsley ordered. He held out the "knitting bag" and prodded the nearest passenger. "Drop your contributions in here and be quick!" he snapped.

Advancing down the aisle, he stripped each passenger of their money, jewelry and other valuables. His pal was following, back to, watching to see that the victims did not attack from the rear.

"Please don't take my watch," one man begged. "It was my father's! It even has his name, 'Richard Birdsong,' engraved on the case! It's really not worth much but it has a lot of sentimental value to me."

"Hand it over and empty your pockets too!" the robber insisted ruthlessly.

By this time Kay had boarded the train. Near the end of the car sat a woman weeping. Kay didn't know her but it so happened that she was a cousin of Chris Eaton's.

"Don't take my ring!" the woman cried. "I'll give you all my money, but let me keep my ring!"

In answer, Beardsley roughly wrenched a lovely sapphire ring from her finger and dropped it gleefully into his sack.

By this time a fast thinking brakeman had locked the door to the adjoining coach. As the thieves rushed across the platform between the two cars, they realized they had been foiled. They quickly jumped down the steps and rushed away into the night.

Someone yelled, "Catch that girl! She's their accomplice!" and suddenly Kay was being yanked by the brakeman.

"The robbers got away," the brakeman explained to the others about him, "but we've got their girl. We'll make her give us some information!"

Kay tried to explain but was gruffly silenced with, "Save that for the police!"

The train started up again but before reaching Clarkville had to make one more unscheduled stop.

This was to shovel off the snow Desrale and Beardsley had piled on the tracks.

Kay was in a daze. She felt first hot, then cold and then everything started to spin.

Word of the robbery had been relayed ahead and when the train finally drew into the station at Clarkville, two policemen were waiting to hustle Kay off to headquarters. Kay felt very ill and didn't have the energy to explain. She just kept muttering again and again:

"I had nothing to do with it."

"For some reason I believe her," said one of the policemen. "She just doesn't look like a thief."

By the time they reached the station both officers felt convinced of Kay's innocence. Nevertheless they were duty bound to bring her before their chief.

"You better take off your shoes and coat first, Miss. They're soaked," said one of the two who had brought her in.

While Kay's wet things were spread out near a heater to dry, a clerk brought her some hot soup.

"Oh, that tastes so good," Kay said weakly.

Presently she was taken to the chief. He questioned her carefully and was convinced by her answers that she had had nothing to do with the robbery.

"I'd like to get in touch with my cousin," said Kay after the police had expressed their apologies. "His name is Bill Tracey and he lives in Brantwood. Can you place the call for me?"

"Of course," the police chief said.

The call was made and Kay was relieved to learn that Bill's two detectives were coming to take her home. It had been an exhausting day and Kay was glad it was nearly over. As it turned out, however, the day and its events were far from over!

Kay had dozed off while waiting and the next thing she knew she was being awakened by one of the policemen. "Here come Tilden and Lee," he said. "You got here in pretty good time," he said to the men.

"Yes, considering this awful weather," Lee said.

"It's a regular blizzard," the other detective added. "I'm frozen stiff."

"As soon as we warm up a bit, Miss Tracey, we'll get going," Lee said.

"Your cousin wants us to check out the old house on our way back. He'll be meeting us there."

Kay didn't dare say so but at that moment she wasn't too interested in the thieves' hide-out. All she could think about was getting home—into a hot bath and a warm bed.

Just as they reached the dreary old place they spotted Bill coming down the lane.

"Pretty good timing," he said as he reached the porch.

Then, as stealthily as burglars, the three men and Kay crept into the house.

This time there were no moans, no creaks or footsteps, no hushed voices. The place was dark and still.

"Let's see what we can find," said the detectives.

Turning on the lights they began an intensive search of the first floor. It revealed nothing.

"Beardsley and Desrale went upstairs when they put their disguises on, so there should be some trace of them there," Kay suggested.

Up the hall steps the searching party went, keeping close together as a precaution. The shabby rooms contained old furniture and had a lived-in appearance. A thorough examination turned up nothing.

"The nest is empty and the birds have flown," Lee remarked.

"Wait a minute!" Kay called excitedly, backing out of a closet with something in her hands.

XIII

An Empty House

———————————◆———————————

"This is the outfit Jack Beardsley wore!" Kay announced, holding up a dress and coat. "And here are the old things Ollie Desrale wore. I'm sure these are Nanna's clothes!"

"If they are, it could mean that the old lady is an accomplice."

"This can all be used as evidence. Let's take it with us," the attorney said, bundling the garments together.

"I was hoping we'd find some of the loot taken from the passengers," Kay said.

"We seem to have found all there is here," Bill said, "and I think we had better get you home, Kay. It's late and you look absolutely worn out."

"I am pretty tired," Kay admitted.

"I'll be glad to get out of this dreary place," Tilden said, heading for the front door.

"We may not have found any of the loot, but," Kay remarked as they left, "at least we have the 'Double Disguise'!"

As soon as Kay got home she phoned Ronald's house to see if he had returned.

"No sign of him, they say," she reported, "and his mother is frantic." Kay turned to Bill and said, "Ronald jumped out of the car to run after those thieves and that was the end of him! What could have happened, Bill?"

"I don't know but we'd better notify the police."

Kay was terribly worried about her friend but reassured by the police who promised to start looking at once.

"Now, that that's done, I want you to get right to bed," said Mrs. Tracey. "You're exhausted and you feel a little feverish."

When Mrs. Tracey checked in on Kay during the night she found her tossing and turning—her head hot and her feet icy. She spoke to their doctor first thing in the morning and he came right over.

"It looks like pneumonia," the doctor said. "However, we've caught it early so there's really nothing to worry about. Just follow my instructions and she'll be over the worst of it soon enough."

Mrs. Tracey had been sitting with Kay for hours when the phone rang. She was delighted to hear Ronald's voice.

"Where are you?" she asked eagerly.

"Home again!" Ronald said.

"Did you get lost in the blizzard? Did the police find you?"

"No, I hitchhiked home after I came to."

"Came to!" Mrs. Tracey cried in alarm.

"What do you mean? What happened?"

"Well, I chased and almost caught up with one of the men, when he whirled around and hit me with the butt of his revolver. You should see my black eye.

"When I came to, I was lying half covered with

snow. The train had left and there wasn't a soul in sight. Kay and the car were gone. It took me forever to hitchhike home, and oh, what a headache I had!" moaned the boy. "I went right to sleep and just woke up. How's Kay?" he asked.

"She's had quite an adventure but I'll let her tell you about that." Mrs. Tracey answered, "Right now she's in bed with pneumonia."

She could hear the boy's quick exclamation and cluck of dismay at the other end of the wire.

"I'm sorry to hear that," Ronald said. "Please tell her I hope she's feeling better soon and if there's anything I can do, just let me know."

While Mrs. Tracey had been on the phone with Ronald, Bill had driven off with Mr. Worth, the twins' father to pick up the Tracey car. However, when they reached the spot where Kay had said she'd left the car, it was nowhere in sight.

"Maybe Ronald took it," Mr. Worth suggested. "Though if he had, you should have heard from him by now."

Phoning Ronald from a nearby house they learned that Ronald knew nothing about the whereabouts of the car.

"There's only one conclusion," Bill said. "The thieves drove it away."

After reporting this latest development to the police, Bill returned to Brantwood. He was delighted to hear Kay was resting easily and had been feeling much better.

"Kay's past the worst of it," the doctor assured the Traceys, the next morning, "but she must be quiet for a few days to avoid a relapse."

Among the people who dropped by to visit Kay were Miss Janey and Doctor Staunton.

Kay thought of Miss Janey as an unromantic, middle-aged person with little interest outside her work and her memories but she was obviously quite taken with Doctor Staunton. Her cheeks had taken on a healthy color, her eyes had lost their melancholy look and now sparkled. She seemed younger and almost pretty. She had certainly found a new interest in life and the interest was clearly as strong on Doctor Staunton's part.

Kay was still thinking about this amazing turn of events when the twins arrived.

"I'd have to see it to believe it," Betty said.

At that point, Wendy burst into verse:

> *"Be not surprised if love blooms late!*
> *Youth does not always find its mate.*
>
> *Remember, underneath the snow*
> *Christmas roses sometimes grow!"*

The three friends talked at length about the budding romance and were still on the subject when another visitor arrived.

The twins left as Mrs. Tracey ushered in Mrs. Dale.

"I was so sorry to hear you've been sick," the woman said timidly. "I've brought you a little present."

Pulling out a jar of jelly from her shopping bag, she held it up to the light at the window.

"See how clear it is. I think it's got a real pretty color and a special flavor. I hope you like it."

"I'm sure I will!" Kay said. "Thank you so much."

"I got the recipe from a good friend of mine, a darling old lady by the name of Lucy Larrop. At least that's her real name but her friends call her Nanna."

Kay was so startled she almost dropped the jelly to the floor!

XIV

The Stolen Formula

Kay was trying to figure out how to get some information from Mrs. Dale without raising her suspicions when, with no prodding whatsoever the woman started talking about her friend.

"I don't know how I ever would have gotten along without her help! Nanna never thinks of herself; she's always helping others, particularly the poor and needy. You can call on her any time of day or night and she'll come right to your bedside and she always knows the right thing to do, too. She knows everything! In fact," she went on with a faraway look, "she knows a good many things other folks don't and she knows how to use her knowledge to very good purpose."

"She sounds like quite a woman," Kay said, encouraging Mrs. Dale to continue.

"She is, although some people say Nanna robs the rich to give to the poor. But I don't believe it. She's so good and kind, I'm sure she's never robbed anybody in her life!"

"Has Nanna ever helped you?" Kay asked.

"I should say so! She's done a lot for me and my children. I don't know how she does it but somehow she always manages to tell me just the right thing to do when I'm in trouble. Folks down our way think she's a regular saint!"

The idea of the old crone being considered "a saint" was too much for Kay. She sank back on her pillows in utter bewilderment.

"I'm afraid Kay is worn out from having so many visitors today," Mrs. Tracey said as she entered the bedroom. "She ought to get some sleep now."

Kay was relieved to see Mrs. Dale go, but not so that she could sleep. She wanted to think over the puzzling things Mrs. Dale had said about Nanna.

Soon after Mrs. Dale left Bill called to say that the police had found the family car.

"Where is it?" Mrs. Tracey asked.

"Someone spotted it stuck in a drift and was good enough to report it to the police. Evidently it was abandoned by the thieves when it ran out of gas. I have it now and I'll be home in it in time for supper."

Bill had scarcely hung up when the telephone rang again. This time it was Mr. Tilden.

"Will you please tell Bill that Lee and I have gone over every inch of the old Larrop place again, but haven't unearthed a single item of any interest."

"Yes, I'll tell him," Mrs. Tracey said.

"We're going to hide in the house awhile," Tilden went on, "in the hopes that someone will show up. If we can catch one of the tenants we'll know more about the train affair."

"I'll tell Bill all of this as soon as he gets home," Mrs. Tracey assured the detective.

Then she tiptoed back to tell Kay. But Kay was sound asleep.

"Poor child! She certainly needs rest!" her mother sighed.

Following the doctor's orders, Mrs. Tracey kept Kay home from school for several more days. One afternoon while her mother was out doing errands Kay amused herself by experimenting in an improvised laboratory in the kitchen. Miss Janey had explained in detail the problems which delayed the perfection of her secret formula and Kay thought she'd try her hand at solving them.

After a couple of hours, Kay thought she'd actually stumbled on something significant.

"Could this simple thing actually be a solution?" she wondered. "Anyhow, it's a step in the process. I'd better go see Miss Janey about it right away."

"I wonder whether Doctor Romeo will be calling on his Juliet!" she laughed to herself as she rang Miss Janey's door bell.

Miss Janey came to the door and Kay was stunned by the contrast between the buoyant happy person of a few days ago and the lifeless woman who stood before her.

What had happened? What could have caused such a change? To Kay's surprise Miss Janey herself brought up the subject.

"I'm in very low spirits, my dear," she began.

"Has something happened?" Kay asked.

Miss Janey's response was to produce a much-creased newspaper clipping.

"This item has upset me very much," she said.

"What is it?" Kay asked.

"It's an article about a chemist who has a formula almost identical to my father's."

She then read the following excerpt from the article.

NEW CHEMICAL DISCOVERY

A new formula of vital interest to industry in the manufacture of acid-resisting textiles has just been worked out by Gustavus Fearson, research chemist.

The Fearson Formula will make practicable a synthetic glass fabric which will not be brittle and easily breakable, but will have a convenient flexibility.

"How do you account for this?" Kay inquired.

"I have no doubt that he got his hands on my father's papers," the woman chemist declared. "However, he will receive credit for the discovery as well as the profit."

"But that's not fair," Kay objected. "We must do something."

"But what?"

Kay marched decisively to the telephone.

XV

Surprises

"WAIT!" Miss Janey cried, springing from her chair. "I don't want you to get yourself into any trouble. I'll—I'll figure out something."

"Don't worry," Kay said. "We're just going to talk to this Mr. Fearson. We've got to get some answers."

The long distance operator quickly put the call through to the unknown chemist. Miss Janey, who had been sick with apprehension for hours, could hardly believe that here in her own house was the voice of the man who had undermined her father's valuable invention. Kay spoke to him in a businesslike way, explaining the whole situation clearly.

"Miss Janey has reason to think you are taking the credit for her father's work and will be turning the matter over to her lawyer!" Kay said sharply to Fearson.

Fearson was amazed and insulted by Kay's accusation. His vehement denials seemed to ring true, but still Kay was skeptical.

"I worked this out honestly and with no idea that

anyone else had discovered the principle," Fearson declared.

"It's hard to believe it's simply coincidence!" Kay cut in critically.

"Why? People frequently hit upon the same idea independently!" the man protested.

"I think you had better come to Miss Janey's at once to clear up this situation," Kay suggested.

"I will!" the chemist said, "and I warn you that I too have a lawyer and I won't hesitate to call him if you persist in these insane accusations!"

"Don't worry," Kay said to Miss Janey. "You won't have any trouble proving your point!"

"Oh, I am not so sure! When my father's papers were stolen, I'm afraid all evidence of my claim to his formula was taken too!"

"Bill will know what to do!" Kay said confidently.

Feeling fully recovered Kay returned to school the next day.

Doctor Staunton seemed to be more absent-minded than usual during chemistry class. Instead of giving the kind of close supervision he was so well known for he fiddled about in a preoccupied manner. In fact, he was so distracted that he neglected to give a homework assignment. Kay mentioned to the twins that their teacher must be in love!

> "*In the spring a young man's fancy*
> *Lightly turns to thoughts of love!*'"

Wendy quoted.

"I wouldn't call him young!" Betty said sharply, "and it's not exactly spring with all that snow on the ground."

"Love makes springtime in the heart," Wendy replied romantically, and Betty groaned.

After school Kay went back to the laboratory to make up work she had missed while she'd been out sick.

"Have you seen Miss Janey since the day we visited you?" Doctor Staunton asked Kay eagerly.

Kay replied that she had, and told him about the chemist who had come up with the same formula worked out by Miss Janey's father.

"He is coming to visit her to discuss the coincidence," Kay said.

The mention of another man visiting Miss Janey seemed to upset the teacher considerably.

"What sort of a person is he?" Doctor Staunton asked.

"I have no idea. We talked only briefly on the phone.

Doctor Staunton paced up and down uneasily and finally dismissed Kay from further work for the day. As she went down the corridor she overheard Chris Eaton talking about the train robbery.

"My cousin Ella Eaton was in it," she announced dramatically, "and she hasn't got over the shock yet. Her life was threatened, all her money and jewelry were stolen. They even got her favorite ring! It was awful," Chris said with exaggerated emotion.

"And to think," she went on, "that Kay was stupid enough to drive those thieves right to the train they were going to hold up. My guess is the men promised her some of the loot. My cousin Ella says she was arrested. That certainly explains why she hasn't shown up at school. She doesn't dare," Chris announced with malicious enthusiasm.

Not wanting to get into an argument with Chris,

Kay quietly slipped away. Ronald, however, and some other boys who had overheard Chris were determined to make the unpleasant girl eat her words.

"Let's take her to the robbers' hideout and give her a good scare," Ronald suggested to his friends.

The boys walked over to Chris and one of them said, "Promise not to tell if we let you in on a secret?"

"I promise," Chris said eagerly.

"We know where the thieves keep their disguises and probably hide their loot."

"Would you like to go with us to investigate the place?" Ronald asked. "Or would you be afraid to go?"

"I'd love to go!" she exclaimed. "Perhaps I could re-capture that blonde thief! Or we might even find the stolen goods!" To herself she added, "That would show Kay she's not so smart!"

"Maybe you'll capture both the robbers and get back all the loot," Ronald encouraged mischievously. "Let's try, anyhow!"

It was arranged that they would all drive out to the old house a half hour later. In the meantime Ronald confided the whole plan to Kay.

"I doubt that we'll find anything interesting. We intend to give Chris a scare though, even if we have to impersonate the robbers ourselves," he chuckled.

Kay immediately told Betty and Wendy about the prank. "Don't you think we ought to trail them to see the fun?" she asked.

"Absolutely, I wouldn't miss it for anything!" Betty replied.

Wendy felt a little conscience-stricken. "Do you think we ought to let them play a trick like that on Chris?" she asked.

"We can keep them from going too far," Kay said.

"In the meantime we might turn up some new evidence at the old house."

Accordingly, when the boys drove off with Chris, Kay and the twins followed at a discreet distance. The boys made much of Chris's bravery and as they expected their compliments swelled her head.

When they reached the house, the boys contrived to get Chris to go in alone. Their plan was to slip around to another entrance and manufacture moans, groans and creeping footsteps. The best laid plans, however, often go wrong, and this one did, in a most unexpected way!

Betty, Wendy and Kay in the meantime had parked nearby the house, but well out of sight. They watched Chris disappear inside the huge, front door. They saw the boys duck around toward the back. Suddenly the air was pierced by a terrible scream!

"What happened?" Betty gasped.

"They've scared her all right!" Kay groaned.

As she raced to the house the thought occured to her that perhaps the boys were not the cause of Chris's scream after all. Maybe the thieves themselves had caught her.

"If anything should happen to her, it will be my fault for letting Ronald pull this prank," Kay told herself.

"Help! Help!" Chris cried.

There was a great commotion inside and then Chris burst out the front door. Two men darted after her.

"Desrale and Beardsley!" Kay thought.

Chris jumped over the railing and fell into the shrubbery below. Both men had pounced on her, when the boys charged from around the corner of the house.

The two men had their hands full as Chris and the boys fought like wild cats. Arriving at the scene of the struggle Kay suddenly shouted:

"Mr. Tilden! Mr. Lee! Stop! These are friends of mine!"

With this the scuffle came to an abrupt stop.

"I forgot you men were hidden in the house!" she said.

"Are you alright, Chris?" Kay asked putting her arm around the girl's shoulders.

"Take your hands off me!" Chris snapped. "This is all your doing, Kay."

XVI

Kay's Suspicion

"This is all my fault! Kay had nothing to do with our coming out here," Ronald explained.

"Yes," one of his friends added, "you are always spreading rumors about Kay and we thought we'd just play a little trick on you to put you in your place!"

"O-o-h!" Chris gasped, stamping her foot in fury.

"Perhaps now you'll be more careful about what you say about Kay," one of the boys added.

"Or it might get all over school that you were scared to death and screamed and ran away!" another boy said.

"You didn't know cops from robbers and Kay had to rescue you!" Ronald said. "What would you have done if you had been alone and had to face the real criminals?"

"You may think all this is very funny," said Tilden, "coming over here and stamping around in a school-boy prank. But you are hindering our efforts to catch the crooks."

"Yes, you certainly are," Lee grumbled. "We'll never catch those two with you young people running around here and scaring them away!" He glowered at the group resentfully.

"This is serious business!" Tilden growled. "Fool around with criminals and you could easily get hurt," he warned sourly.

"It was foolish of us," Kay acknowledged, "and we're sorry," Kay said speaking for the group. "Before we leave, I'd like to talk to you privately for a moment."

Speaking alone to the detectives, Kay related the news regarding the chemist, Gus Fearson, and his development of the very formula which had been stolen. This information instantly put the men in better spirits.

"This could be a big help," Tilden exclaimed. "Thanks for the tip."

"Fearson is coming to Miss Janey's today and I'll let you know what we find out." Kay promised.

"Meanwhile we'll go back to our dreary watch," Lee grumbled. "It's very dull sitting in that house all day, never seeing a soul! We haven't even laid eyes on your friend Nanna!"

"Well, goodbye and good luck!" Kay called as they separated, the detectives returning to their posts and the students to town.

"Drop me off at Miss Janey's on the way back," Kay requested of the twins. "Fearson should be there by now and I want to meet him."

Fearson was a serious young man, with a straightforward way about him. He stated again that in no way had he been dishonest about the work and seemed quite sincere.

"How could you have hit upon exactly the same

formula as the one stolen from me?" Miss Janey demanded.

"I don't blame you for asking, and I'll tell you just how it happened."

"Some time ago I was approached by a young woman who wanted to rent part of my laboratory. She offered to pay me a fee for my advice on some work. I consented. After a while she hit upon a series of experiments which resulted in part of the formula with which you are familiar."

"She probably didn't discover anything!" Kay said indignantly. "She had the stolen papers all the time and simply copied them!"

"Possibly," the chemist assented who obviously was puzzled about the affair. "I admit that she was no chemist. She couldn't seem to go any further with her experiments and agreed to turn the development of the thing over to me with the understanding that we were to share the profits."

"I wonder whether she could be the same young woman who pried into my affairs at the bank?" said Miss Janey.

"More than likely," Kay agreed. "What arrangement did you make with her, Mr. Fearson?"

"All patents were to be taken out in my name," he answered, "but I am to pay her royalties for the use of her part of the discovery. This seemed fair enough, for the invention is sure to be of great importance. Everything seemed to be going well until you called me and challenged my right to the formula. Frankly, I don't know what to make of it."

"It's clear enough!" Kay declared. "That girl had the stolen Janey formula!"

"She must have recognized its value," Miss Janey

said thoughtfully, "and had learned that it could not be put to use without developing other chemical compounds."

"I suppose it's possible," the young man replied.

"Can you describe the woman?" Kay asked.

"Oh, yes. Slender, medium height, always very neatly and fashionably dressed. I particularly remember her voice which was almost unnaturally high pitched."

"Did she have particularly big feet?" Kay asked with a smile.

"Well, I'm afraid I never noticed," the young man said apologetically. "To tell the truth I am not very observant about ladies."

"What was her name?" Kay pressed further.

"Adele Cortiz. I remember wondering why anyone with so Spanish a name could be so blonde. To me the name suggests a dark-haired, dark-eyed beauty. Miss Cortiz on the other hand is very fair and no beauty!"

"Sounds exactly like Jack Beardsley in disguise!" Kay thought to herself, "but perhaps I had better not mention that just yet."

At this point the doorbell rang loudly. Jessie Hipple pattered from the kitchen to open it and in strode Doctor Staunton. He glared for a moment at the younger chemist as Miss Janey murmured an introduction, addressed a few words pleasantly to Kay, then seated himself as near his hostess as possible.

Kay instinctively felt that she was not needed or perhaps even wanted, so she excused herself. Passing by the laboratory she was surprised to find it lighted. Someone was in the room; Kay couldn't see anyone but she could hear them. Then Jessie's head appeared above a desk.

"Oh, it's you, Miss Tracey!"

Bending down again, the maid was closely examining the floor.

"Did you lose something? Can I help?" Kay offered.

Jessie gave no direct answer but warned Kay to be careful of the valuable equipment.

"We don't want any more accidents like that fire the other time you were in here!" she said sharply.

Jessie continued to search on the floor and mumbled a few words indistinctly about having dropped something. So peculiar was the girl's behavior that Kay became suspicious and forced a straight answer from her.

"Well, if you must know," the maid grumbled, "I knocked over one of those little test tubes there and I want to get up all the glass."

A glance at the tube rack showed Kay that the ingredient which Jessie must have spilled was a poison. Before she could ask another question the culprit had left the room.

"This strong acid will eat holes in the floor," Kay thought. "I'd better get something and wash it up or Jessie will be in trouble. I can't imagine why she was tampering with these test tubes."

XVII

The Escape

Kay quickly went to work, mopping the acid with a cleaner. While the girl was busy working, the door swung open and in walked Miss Janey.

"Why, what are you doing, Kay?" she asked in surprise.

Kay looked up from the floor. Rising, wet rag in hand, the girl replied, "Jessie spilled some acid and I was mopping it up before it cuts holes in your floor."

"What was she doing in here?" asked Miss Janey somewhat bewildered. "And why should she be handling acids or anything else?"

"I don't know," Kay answered. "Perhaps she was dusting."

"Well, never mind," the woman said dubiously. "Mr. Fearson has gone and Doctor Staunton and I have reached an agreement with him for the time being. We'd like to tell you about it, so you can take the matter up with your cousin."

Kay washed her hands, then followed Miss Janey into the living room where Doctor Staunton explained the arrangement with Mr. Fearson.

"He will get in touch with this Miss Cortiz and then

let us know where we can find her. Then we'll arrive with the police to question her and perhaps secure her arrest if evidence warrants it."

"It looks as if we're closing in on those rascals at last!" Kay exclaimed.

"I hope so," Miss Janey said.

"Don't worry about a thing!" Doctor Staunton said. "Just leave it to us and your ownership of the formula will be established."

Fearson was an honest man. He would never have cheated anyone and he was indignant that he had been suspected of doing so. Gazing out the window on the train ride home, he went over the whole situation in his mind.

The more he thought about it, the more angry he became that he had been made a tool for Cortiz's dishonest scheme.

By the next morning he was so over-wrought and furious at the very thought of the Cortiz girl, that he forgot the importance of proceeding carefully. Impatient to trap her into a confession and hand her over to the law, he went directly to her hotel and accused her point blank of stealing the formula.

"How dare you make these accusations," cried the woman indignantly.

"How dare you involve me in a crooked scheme," the chemist retorted.

With this the woman slumped in her chair and covered her face with a handkerchief, sobbing gently into it.

"Oh, how can you say such dreadful things!" she said. "It just goes to show it's a man's world and if a woman tries to compete in it her professional standing is questioned."

Poor Gus wasn't sure how to handle the situation.

"Mr. Fearson," Miss Cortiz said through her tears, "I am dreadfully upset by all this, as you can see. Would you mind waiting for me down here while I go to my room and lie down for a few minutes. I am sure we can straighten out the whole thing. I'd be only too glad to go with you to see these people who so misunderstand me."

She spoke so convincingly that Fearson was more bewildered than ever. Could he be wrong about her after all?

"I'll wait," he agreed, "but not for long. If those people don't get a satisfactory explanation right away they'll start proceedings against both of us!"

"I won't be long," the woman assured him.

Fearson waited for some time, impatiently checking his watch every few minutes. He waited and waited, but Miss Cortiz did not return.

So intent was Fearson on getting a confession out of the woman that he failed to notice certain interesting things about her. Not only were her feet unusually large but her hands were thick and crude as they protruded from her dainty sleeves. Miss Cortiz had, it is true, a rosey complexion, thanks to a clever bit of make-up, but the texture of her skin was coarse.

Adele Cortiz was none other than the sly Jack Beardsley! Back in the room he hurriedly removed his disguise and slipped on trousers and a jacket.

He dashed down the stairs and slipped quietly out of a side door, and fled up a side street.

By the time Gus began to suspect that something was wrong, the culprit had vanished completely! Anyone following him would be looking for a young woman, so, with this disguise carried in his suitcase, he felt comparatively safe.

The discouraged Fearson took an express train

back to Brantwood. There he met with Miss Janey, Bill and the two detectives. All listened attentively to the chemist's story.

"I'm sure that was Beardsley!" Tilden said. "Too bad he got away again."

"Do you think we've lost him for good this time?" Miss Janey asked.

"No, on the contrary he has made it easier for us to trace him," Bill said. "I suggest that you and Mr. Fearson come to some sort of temporary agreement without going to the law about it. Unless I am seriously mistaken, this gentleman is honest and willing to cooperate with us."

"Absolutely!" Fearson assured them.

With that Bill drew up a tentative arrangement. "This is to withhold the product from the market until certain facts are determined in the case," he explained.

"It seems satisfactory to me," Miss Janey said after a careful reading of the document.

"To me also," Fearson agreed.

"In that case you can both sign here on the dotted lines."

"I want you all to come home and have dinner with us," Mrs. Tracey urged as the business matter was being concluded.

The invitation broke the tension under which everyone had been and the entire group drove to the Tracey's where a good meal and pleasant conversation took everyone's mind off the unsolved case.

During the desert the phone rang and Bill jumped up to answer it.

"This is Jessie Hipple!" the girl said urgently.

"What's the matter, Jessie?"

"There's a burglar in the house! Oh, please come as quickly as you can! I'm so scared! Please hurry!"

XVIII

The Phantom Burglar

With this startling piece of news, everyone at the dinner table tumbled into the Traceys' car and Bill then drove at top speed to Miss Janey's.

As they came in sight of the house, they saw Jessie standing on the porch.

"Oh, I'm so glad you're here!" she cried. "I'm freezing out here and I'm afraid to go in! There's a man inside."

"What makes you think so?" asked Bill who had been through false alarms before with jumpy people.

"I saw him!" Jessie declared. "At least I saw his shadow! A big, stocky sort of man, slightly round shouldered! Oh, my heart beat so hard I thought it would burst!"

"There's nobody here!" Bill scoffed after they'd searched the house.

"Well, there was!" Jessie insisted.

"Did you look in the basement?" Fearson asked.

"I have and there's nobody there," Tilden reported.

"Maybe he stole all the silver or something and ran

away with it!" the maid said, but nothing seemed to have been stolen.

Inclined to believe that Jessie's extreme fright had some real foundation Kay prowled around alone for a while. On a hunch she went to check out the laboratory.

"It might not be the family silver that the burglar was after," she said to herself.

Then she spotted something lying on a little shelf, next to a bottle labelled "poison," was a man's glove! She asked Miss Janey and Jessie about it but neither could account for its being there.

"Now you see! I told you a man had been here!" Jessie cried. "What if he comes back at night when Miss Janey and I are here all alone!"

"Now, Jessie," Miss Janey said, "if I'm not afraid, you needn't be either."

Kay was wondering about the possible significance of the glove being next to the poison. She was sure it was the same poison Jessie had dropped the day before. Could there be any connection.

Her thoughts were interrupted by the ringing of the doorbell. Jessie, glad of an excuse to be busy, hurried to the hall. It occured to Kay when she saw the caller that he answered the maid's description of the burglar! He was "big, stocky, and slightly round shouldered!"

"But this is Doctor Staunton!" she said to herself.

"Well, well!" Staunton said heartily, "here you all are, and when I came a little while ago there was no one at home."

"You were here before?" Miss Janey asked in surprise.

"Yes, I rang and no one answered. I went around to the side and found the laboratory door unlocked. I went in but no one seemed to be home so I left. I drove up the road to a gas station and on my way back I saw you through the window and thought I would stop by!"

"I'm glad you did," Miss Janey said.

"I had given up hope of seeing you this evening," the teacher said turning attentively to her.

"We were having dinner at the Traceys'," Miss Janey explained, "when Jessie telephoned that there was a burglar in the house!"

"So we all came to catch him!" Mrs. Tracey laughed.

"Oh, I must have frightened poor Jessie when I came in the side door!" the man said apologetically.

"Is this your glove?" Kay asked, extending it to him.

"Yes, I must have left it here. I wondered what had happened to it."

"So you are the phantom burglar!" Miss Janey laughed.

Jessie blushed in embarrassment. "Anyway I'll be able to sleep tonight," she sighed, bustling back into the kitchen.

"Come, Kay," Mrs. Tracey said, "you have some homework to get to. What will Doctor Staunton say if you are not prepared for his chemistry class?"

The teacher and his pupil exchanged smiles, and Kay followed her mother, Bill, Gus Fearson and the detectives to the car.

"We'll drop you off at the station," Bill said to Fearson. "You'll be just in time for the next train. If you can get on the trail of your friend Adele Cortiz, let us know at once!"

"I'll do my best," the man promised weakly, reminded of his former failure.

"Don't be discouraged!" Bill said. "You'll trap her—or rather him—yet!"

"I hope so," the other returned grimly, as he swung up the steps of the train.

Paying particular attention to chemistry, Kay stayed up late that night to do her homework. She was so well prepared in chemistry the next day that Doctor Staunton asked her to stay after class and help some of the students who were behind in their work.

"Goody!" Betty whispered to Kay. "I'm sure you'll make the subject more understandable to me than he does!"

Chris Eaton of course resented Kay's presence and went ahead with an experiment by herself.

"Oh, Chris!" Kay cried a little later, as she observed what the girl was doing. "I don't mean to interfere but what you're doing isn't safe. It could blow up!"

"I don't need you to teach me!"

Chris turned her back on Kay, fussed around with some equipment for a few minutes, then abruptly left the room. There was a sly look on her face.

Shortly afterward came the sudden pop of a slight explosion, followed by smoke and the tinkle of broken glass. Whirling around to see what had happened Kay saw a small fire.

"Chris did this and she did it on purpose!" Kay murmured.

"Of course she did!" Wendy said flying to the rescue with Betty.

Together the girls beat out the fire.

"If anyone sees this, it will look like we are to blame for the accident!" Kay said.

"I'm sure that was the idea," Betty agreed furiously.

"Here comes someone now!" Wendy cried.

Sure enough, heavy footsteps thudded down the

hall and turned in at the laboratory door. There stood Mr. Preston, the high school principal!

He stopped, stared, sniffed, then hastily strode over to the black, smouldering mass which the girls were extinguishing.

"What's going on here?" he demanded.

Wendy tried to explain but the principal was so annoyed that he wouldn't let her finish.

"Yes, yes! Very careless," he said sharply. "Let me see what the damage is."

As he peered over the table the lights suddenly went out! In the semi-dark room Kay tried to clear away the charred mess but misjudged her distance and ended up knocking over a box of white powder.

The powder had been on a shelf just above the principal's head and when Kay knocked it over it sprinkled all over the man powdering him from head to foot. It even blew into his eyes and nose.

"What are you girls up to?" the principal cried angrily. "How dare you abuse school property? And what is this stuff you have thrown all over me?" he asked, fumbling for his handkerchief.

Wendy and Betty could hardly keep from laughing, but not Kay. Knowing what the powder was, she was afraid it would damage the man's sight.

XIX

A Lucky Accident

Drawn by the ruckus the janitor was soon on the scene and within minutes he replaced the burned out fuse.

As the lights went on, the sight of Mr. Preston, white with powder, drew hushed laughter from the group.

"A double disguise!" snickered Betty to Kay.

Kay's insistence that he wash the chemical from his skin and his eyes immediately sent him hurriedly off to the washroom. When he emerged Kay asked about his eyes and was relieved when he said they felt only slightly irritated.

The next day Wendy, Betty and Kay were summoned to Mr. Preston's office and reprimanded. Betty was angry that Chris, the real culprit, was not sharing the punishment. Kay would not tattle on the girl but without giving any names, Betty made it clear that someone else was to blame for the fire. She added that Kay had been asked to stay in the laboratory to help others.

Mr. Preston spoke at length about the dangers of playing with chemicals and the importance of responsible behavior. As an aside he added that the white powder was so powerful it had changed the color of his clothes.

Kay couldn't get her mind off the strange effect the powder had on the principal's clothes.

"I'm going to try that out on some cloth as soon as I can get to Miss Janey's laboratory," she decided. "Perhaps—" and a gleam came into her eyes as a plan flashed into her mind.

Kay wasted no time in getting to Miss Janey's and starting her experiment. Carefully she mixed a little of the powder with a red fluid, then with a green one and finally with a colorless liquid.

"Doctor Staunton would be the first one to approve of my trying this," she thought as she watched the various mixtures.

She then shook a liberal amount of the powder over an old piece of cloth. Anxiously she awaited results. At first nothing happened. Then gradually the color of the cloth changed.

"So far so good. Now for the exciting part!" she said.

Drop by drop she added the liquids in the test tubes to various sections of the cloth. As they mingled with the fabric, other changes than those of color took place!

"The texture of the cloth is changing!" she cried in delight. "One's getting rubbery, one's spongy, this other is—oh hurrah!"

Finding Miss Janey in her library chatting with Doctor Staunton, Kay excitedly told them both about her experiment. They were fascinated and all three raced back to the laboratory.

They worked enthusiastically together until nightfall modifying and repeating the experiment. Finally Doctor Staunton and Miss Janey straightened up from their absorbing tasks.

"We've done it!" Miss Janey exulted. "This is the missing link needed to perfect my father's invention! In fact, your discovery, Kay, is better than the original!"

Kay blushed with pleasure.

"It's similar, but infinitely better!" Doctor Staunton added.

"How did you hit upon it?" the woman scientist asked.

"By accident," Kay said and told Miss Janey about the incident in the school laboratory, which of course Doctor Staunton knew about.

"You were quick to see its possibilities!" he congratulated.

"Now we are independent of the Fearson Formula!" Miss Janey rejoiced. "If I fail to get all patent rights preventing his infringement, it won't matter now!"

"No," the professor agreed, "for here we have an entirely new method, based on the old Janey formula idea, but vastly improved. It ought to be worth a fortune!"

"And you, Kay, are entitled to a generous share of that money," Miss Janey declared, "and you too, Doctor Staunton. Kay had a part in discovering a new process and you in developing it!

"It's wonderful!" Miss Janey cried as she worked on. "See this material. It is as clear as glass, and will not break or tear easily."

"You can make a sheet of it like a transparent tablecloth of any color and as tough as muslin!" Doctor Staunton exulted.

Mrs. Tracey and Bill were asked over and there was a great celebration.

Later that evening old Nanna crept to Miss Janey's door to congratulate her.

"How in the world did you hear about it?" Miss Janey asked. "Not a soul knew it but the Tracey's and Doctor Staunton!"

"I know many things," the old woman cackled. "Nothing is hidden from me! And now I will reveal the future for you!"

She made some strange movements with her hands and a faraway look came into her eyes.

"I see prosperity ahead for you! Wealth and great happiness! The happiness does not seem to rise from wealth. No. I seem to see the figure of a man——"

Miss Janey moved and this seemed to break the spell.

"The vision fades," said the old woman blinking and turning to go.

At that moment Kay arrived at Miss Janey's. Seeing the witch-like visitor walking toward the road, she decided to stop her and ask some questions.

"Pardon me, Mrs. Larrop, but I need your help."

The woman looked surprised but did not speak.

"It's very important that I get some information about your house in the woods," the girl went on.

"Why should I tell you about my affairs?"

"Because your home is being used by thieves as a hide-out," Kay explained. "If you know everything, you must know that! You must be aware also that the police are investigating the place. Won't you help us clear up the mystery?"

Nanna gave Kay a piercing stare, then walked past her in silence. Kay followed and tried again.

"Please help us! Otherwise you may be arrested

and forced to testify in court! Did you know that poor Mrs. Dale has been robbed of everything by people living in that house?"

At this Nanna seemed quite troubled.

"Some people think you are in partnership with the thieves who live there! It's giving you a bad name whether you deserve it or not!" Kay went on.

"I own the house, true," Nanna croaked. "I rent it. But I never condone crime!"

"Then why do you rent your house to thieves?" challenged the girl.

"I had no intention of it being so used," she went on. "I rented it in good faith to a man by the name of Mentor Tryson. He said he wanted a quiet place in the country for his invalid sister. Now I have reason to believe these tenants are crooks. If this is so—!" She raised her thin arms above her head in a threatening gesture. "Let them beware! A fate worse than imprisonment awaits them!"

With this prophecy, the old woman shuffled away.

"She gives me the shivers!" Kay thought.

The next day when Kay went to Mrs. Dale's she heard more about Nanna's good deeds.

"You can't imagine how good old Nanna is to us! Why, I would have been put out of this little house into the snow, without a roof over the children's heads, if it had not been for her!"

"What do you mean?" asked Kay.

"I couldn't pay my rent and the landlord was going to put me out. Somehow Nanna learned about it and paid the bill for me. I never would have known who it was if the landlord hadn't told me. How can I ever thank her?"

"She's a strange character!" Kay said.

"She's an angel!" Mrs. Dale declared emphatically.

"I can't picture an angel running a den for thieves," Kay said later to the twins. "That woman must have been aware of the use those men were making of her place and her clothes!

"Let's go out to the house one more time," Kay proposed. "We can take a look at the robbers' car. It may give us some clues, remember Ronald and I ditched it the night of the blizzard. I'm pretty sure it's still stuck there."

"Let's go!" Betty agreed.

"I hope we don't get into more trouble," Wendy said.

As the girls crept up the lane to the old house Betty cried, "Look, someone is working on that car now! Maybe it's one of the robbers!"

XX

The Poison Vial

The girls hid behind some thick shrubbery and watched as the robbers' car was put into running order. As soon as all four wheels were on firm ground again, and the engine running smoothly, a man slid into the seat. He pulled out a wallet, paid the wreckers and drove off.

He quickly passed the girls but Kay got a good look at him. The man wore horn-rimmed glasses and his face was smudged with car grease. He was dressed like a laborer, in thick sweater with heavy overalls pulled up over it, and a woolen cap with ear tabs pulled down.

"I thought I recognized that man," she gasped minutes later.

"That man was Ollie Desrale, Jack Beardsley's partner." "I thought those thieves were both blonde!" Wendy said bewildered.

"Yes," said Betty, "and this man seemed dark and swarthy."

"Don't you see?" Kay said. "He was disguised. His appearance was very cleverly altered, but I am positive that was Ollie. I'll never forget that long foxy nose of his and those cruel eyes!"

Kay stopped the wrecker as it passed and questioned the driver. "Can you tell me the name of the man whose car you just fixed?"

"No. He phoned us to come and pull him out of here and we did. Then he paid us. That's all we know about him."

As the wrecker vanished down the road, Tilden and Lee came along. When Kay told them what had just happened, the men decided to try and follow him.

"Here's the license number!" Kay said handing Tilden a slip of paper from her purse.

Deciding that nothing more could be accomplished just then at the old house, the three girls got in their car and headed for home.

"Let's visit Miss Janey!" Kay suggested, as they rode along.

"Oh, I'm so glad you're here!" Miss Janey said when the girls arrived. "I'm terribly upset and don't know what to do!"

"What's happened?" Kay asked with concern.

"Someone has broken into the laboratory and stolen a vial of deadly poison which I had there for experimental purposes!"

"*Who* could it have been?" Kay asked.

"I just don't know," the agitated woman answered.

"Do you think someone is deliberately planning to poison——"

"I hope not!" Miss Janey gasped.

"Where was it kept?"

Miss Janey pointed to a place on a shelf.

"That's the very spot where I found Doctor Staunton's glove the night of Jessie's phantom burglar scare!" Kay cried.

Miss Janey immediately phoned to Doctor Staunton to see if he had taken the vial for any reason. However he said he hadn't and was as mystified about its disappearance as the others.

"Could Nanna have taken it?" Kay asked.

"Oh, no!" Miss Janey declared positively. "There is no reason to suspect her!"

Kay was not so sure. When she and the twins resumed their ride home, all three discussed this possibility.

"She's so weird. Nothing she could do would surprise me!" Betty remarked.

"But is she as evil as she seems?" Kay questioned. "That's what I can't decide after hearing Mrs. Dale praise her."

"Nanna may want to avenge herself on the tenants of her house," Kay said. "She threatened them with a 'fate worse than imprisonment!'"

Another horrible thought popped into her mind but she decided not to mention it to the twins. What if Nanna sets a poison trap in the house to kill the robbers and Tilden and Lee are poisoned by mistake? After the girls had left her, Kay continued to worry about this.

"I think I'll visit Mrs. Dale and see if she can throw any light on Nanna's recent activities," she resolved.

Not wanting to go empty handed Kay brought some soup and a cake and the whole family glowed with appreciation.

"Where's Teddy?" Kay asked, looking about for the older brother.

A sad look came over the mother's face. "My Teddy's never at home much these days," she sighed, her eyes filling with tears.

"Why not?"

"He says it's not like home any more. He tells me

he's a poor child out trying to make some money!" answered Mrs. Dale. "He keeps saying he's tired of being poor and he won't stand it any longer. It frightens me to have him talk that way," said the widow with a sob that worried the other children.

"Oh, don't worry about him, he'll be all right," Kay comforted her.

"I'm so afraid he'll do something stupid. He might steal! If he did anything like that, I couldn't bear it!"

"Teddy isn't going to do anything wrong, I'm sure of it!" Kay persisted.

"Oh, he might!" Mrs. Dale cried. "I tell him we may be poor but we must be honest, and he says that he doesn't see why! He's been very difficult and insolent lately and I can't handle him! If only his father hadn't died and left me to struggle alone with all these problems."

The poor woman wiped away her tears on the baby's blanket.

With a comforting pat on the shoulder from Kay the widow went on:

"Teddy worries me so! Just before he went out today I found the strangest looking bottle in his pocket. It was marked 'POISON.' When I asked him about it he just snatched it away and ran out without a word."

"Where did he go?" Kay asked excitedly.

"I don't know."

"What did the bottle look like?" Kay asked, trying not to let the boy's mother see how alarmed she was.

"It was a small blue vial. It had a red label with a picture of a skull and crossbones on it and the word POISON in big black letters. Underneath it told what to do in case of poisoning. Teddy snatched the bottle away before I could read the name on it."

Kay said goodbye to Mrs. Dale and the children and quickly drove home.

"I've got to tell Bill about this right away," she thought apprehensively. "I'm sure Teddy got that poison from Miss Janey's laboratory. I hate to think what he may be planning to do with it."

XXI

Skates, Skis, Sleuths!

———————————◆———————————

Bill was extremely disturbed about Teddy's possession of the poison.

"He's definitely up to something! I hope we can find him before it's too late," Bill said.

"Maybe Teddy is going after the men who swindled his mother," Kay suggested.

"He may even know where those crooks are!" Bill added.

"Which is more than anybody else knows!" Kay said.

Bill and Kay looked all over town for Teddy but there was no sign of him. Not even a clue as to his whereabouts.

"Morning may bring a different story," Bill said to the discouraged girl.

In the morning, however, the situation was just as bleak. Mrs. Dale reported that Teddy had not come home all night. The detective had not found the thief who had got away in his car. His accomplice also still eluded the search of the police.

It was late in the day when a ray of light filtered through the dark puzzle. In connection with her school work Kay was supposed to see a certain movie about the life of a great scientist. Kay decided to go that evening and asked her mother, Bill and Miss Janey to go with her.

As they were coming out of the theater, Bill spotted the manager in the lobby.

"Any word about your film operator?" Bill asked.

"Not one," the manager responded. "Actually something interesting did turn up the other day, but I don't know how much it is worth."

"What was that?" Kay asked alertly.

"We ran a newsreel and I declare if it didn't show a picture of our Beardsley right among some other people!"

"What was it?" Bill asked.

"It was one showing winter sports; skating, skiing, and all that sort of thing, up at Lake Diamond."

"Where did you see Beardsley?" Kay asked.

"Well, at one point the reel showed a crowd watching a ski jump. As sure as I stand here Jack Beardsley was in that crowd! He probably went up there to pick people's pockets!"

"Did you send anyone there to try to catch him?" Bill asked.

"No. I figured he'd be gone by the time anyone got up there. He may be all the way down to Florida by now!" The manager scowled with the thought of the hopelessness of catching the man.

Kay was not so easily discouraged. On the way home she said; "Wasn't it lucky we went to the movies? We finally got a clue to Jack's whereabouts! Oh, Mother, I'd like to spend Saturday at Lake Diamond with Betty and Wendy. Is that alright?"

"Why do you want to go up there just now?" Mrs. Tracey asked.

"Oh, for fun partly, and also to do a little business," Kay laughed. "We would look for Beardsley!"

"I hate to say no," Mrs. Tracey said, "but I am awfully worried about you girls getting into trouble. You do seem to have a knack for getting in the most unexpected scrapes. I'd go with you on Saturday but I have an important appointment. Well, I know how important this is to you. I guess if it's alright with Mrs. Worth, it's alright with me."

Saturday morning the girls caught the early train for Lake Diamond. It was a beautiful day and the train was full with people going up for the day.

The girls could hardly wait to reach the scene. They chattered merrily on the ride, peering out of the windows at the snow-clad landscape.

"I just hope Jack Beardsley is still there!" Kay said to her friends.

"I have a feeling he will be," Betty replied confidently.

"I hope you're right!" said Wendy. "Anyway here we are and we'll soon find out!"

"Look who's getting off the train, Mr. Tilden!" Betty exclaimed.

"Bill told him about the clue in the newsreel," Kay explained as she waved to the man.

As Tilden came over, Kay asked, "Up here to trap Jack Beardsley?"

"I'll get him if I can," he answered, "but ten to one the scoundrel has flown to a warmer climate. I hope he has, then I'd be sent to a warm spot after him! This cold is no fun for me. I'd rather be basking in the sunshine."

The girls couldn't help laughing at the detective's intolerance for what was to them invigorating winter weather.

"I'll be glad when this case breaks, if it ever does!"

he grumbled. "I've been hiding in Lucy Larrop's old cellar for days now and caught nothing but a cold. Now here I am on another wild goose chase! I tell you, hunting criminals is a terrible way to earn one's living! As soon as I can I'm going to retire and live on a farm where nothing ever happens!"

The girls left the disgruntled detective still mumbling about his hard lot, and went to the hotel to make a lunch reservation.

"Let's look through the register. Maybe Jack Beardsley or Adele Cortiz are listed."

They checked the register but there was nothing to give a clue to Beardsley's possible presence.

"Naturally he wouldn't register in his own name," Wendy said.

"You're right. He'd give a false name," Betty said, "and probably even disguise his handwriting."

"True," agreed Kay, "but I feel sure he's still up here. There are so many wealthy people at this resort. You'd think he'd stick around awhile to rob as many of them as possible. He'd have to stay somewhere and this is the only hotel."

"We'll keep our eyes open," Betty said, looking around.

At that moment the girls spotted an all too familiar figure, arguing disagreeably with the hotel clerk.

"Chris Eaton, making a fuss as usual!" Kay whispered.

Chris's aunt, Mrs. Pinty, was shrilly adding her dissatisfaction to that of Chris.

"It seems to me that for what we pay, we ought to get better service!"

With that she stalked off, nose in air. Chris with a snippy expression, followed her. Behind their backs the clerk raised his eyebrows and shook his head in disbelief.

"Apparently he feels the way we do about them!" Kay commented.

As she turned to go out, she saw Tilden coming in.

"Any luck?" she asked.

"None," he grunted.

"Well," said Betty to Kay and Wendy. "Even if we don't catch any crooks—there's no reason why we can't have a good time."

The girls went out into the dazzling sunshine and joined the lively throng.

"A skating race! What fun!" Betty cried, edging forward to see the contestants better.

Observers were packed so closely along the roped-off area that the girls became separated in the crowd. However, Kay did not notice this for her attention had suddenly become focused on one particular skater.

XXII

Captured

Teddy Dale was the skater who had attracted Kay's attention. She couldn't believe her eyes. What was he doing in the race?

Excitedly Teddy was trying his best to win the race. So caught up in the race was Kay that for a moment she forgot she'd been looking for the boy. Eagerly she watched him sprinting across the ice.

"Oh, I hope he wins!" thought Kay. "Only a little farther! Oh, good! He's putting distance between himself and the others! He's going to win."

Kay gave a loud cheer as the Dale boy shot across the finish line.

The announcer was calling through a megaphone: "Mile race for juniors won by Theodore Dale!"

After a hearty applause, the man went on, "Ted, it gives me great pleasure to award you first prize for your excellent speed in a well-skated race."

Teddy beamed with pride as the announcer handed him his cash prize. It wasn't much but it was all his. He had won it through his own efforts and that made it very special.

Kay eagerly pushed through the crowd toward the elated boy.

"Teddy! Congratulations!" she greeted the boy. "You were terrific!"

Then she led him aside and asked if his mother knew where he was. Teddy did not reply, and Kay knew from the way he hung his head and dug the tip of one skate nervously in the snow that the answer was "no."

"Teddy, tell me, where is the bottle you took from Miss Janey's laboratory?" Kay asked him suddenly.

"What bottle?" Teddy asked nervously.

"I think you know what I'm talking about. The bottle contains poison and we're all afraid you could get into trouble with it."

Realizing it was futile to play dumb any longer, Teddy answered sullenly, "Nanna wouldn't let me keep it. She made me give it to her."

"How did Nanna know you had it?"

"She knows everything," he answered matter-of-factly.

"What did she want it for?" To herself Kay thought, "It might be more dangerous in her hands than in his."

"I don't know," the boy replied grumpily.

"What were you going to do with it?"

"Nothin'," he said.

"Why did you come up here? To skate?"

"Naw," the boy replied. "I saw a newsreel in the movies and in it as plain as day was the man who took my mother's money. So I got a ride up here on a truck. I want to find that man and get her money back."

"Teddy," said Kay, opening her purse and taking out some money, "I want you to take the first train home. Your mother is frantic about you. Please do as I say, you have my promise that the thief will be caught."

The boy took the money mumbled a few words of thanks and disappeared into the crowd. Suddenly it dawned on Kay that she had become separated from the twins.

Unable to find them, Kay headed back to the hotel to make some phone calls.

"Ride, Miss? Ride back to the hotel?" asked a man driving a sleigh.

Since she was in a hurry, Kay hopped into the sleigh yet no sooner had they taken off than Kay had an uneasy feeling that all was not well.

The driver, huddled in a bulky coat seemed like a sinister figure in the midst of bright sunshine and sparkling snow. He wore dark glasses against the glare from the snow and a big fur hat. He sat hunched over, and every now and then cracked his whip against the horses more sharply than seemed necessary.

"Why, he's not driving back to the hotel at all! He's driving away from it!" Kay realized suddenly.

Trotting swiftly along a road that wound up the side of a mountain bordering the lake, the driver urged the horses on faster with cruel lashes of his whip.

Suddenly he yelled angrily at the horses to urge them on even faster and something in the tone of his voice revealed his identity to Kay.

"It's Ollie Desrale!" she gasped. "Where is he taking me?"

Ahead rose the mountain, its sides dark and shadowy with towering fir trees. The country here was lonely and deserted. Kay peered longingly down at the people at the resort but this scene was now fast vanishing in the distance and people had become mere specks.

Cruelly Desrale thrashed his team as if to put more distance between him and the crowds at Lake Diamond, before the girl could object.

The horses, restive under the whip, had plunged wildly ahead. As they careened around a dangerous hairpin turn, Kay cried, "Just where are you going? Take me back to the hotel at once!"

"Sit down and shut up!" Desrale growled. "You'll soon see where we're going! Sit down, I say!" he bellowed, for Kay had stood up and was about to leap from the sleigh.

She was nervously watching the roadside for a snowy drift in which to jump, when Desrale reached out to stop her. In doing so, he pulled heavily on one rein causing the team to go dangerously near the mountain ledge. As the sleigh nearly overturned, Kay jumped off, falling into the soft snow. On raced the horses, now unmanageable. As Desrale pulled angrily on the reins, the agitated animals reared and slipped. Over the mountainside plunged the ill-fated sleigh!

There was the roar of sliding snow, the wild whinny of terrified animals, echoing cries from Desrale, and a jangle of bells.

Kay walked to the spot where the sleigh had slipped but was afraid to look down.

"Help! Help!" came a weak cry from below.

"He's alive! I've got to try and help him," Kay thought.

A gruesome sight greeted her as she looked over the side of the cliff. The ground was strewn with the tangled wreckage of the smashed sleigh. The injured horses, trapped in their own harness, were clearly in agony. Not another word came from the man who had caused this calamity.

"I must get down there but how I don't know."

Kay's dilemma was interrupted by the welcome sound of sleigh bells.

"Someone's coming!" Kay breathed in relief.

She was about to yell for help when the horrible thought struck her that perhaps this was Jack Beardsley following his partner! She crouched low under a bushy evergreen. The sleigh came to a halt and a man came trudging to the edge of the road.

With a sudden cry of delight Kay scrambled from her hiding place. "Oh, Mr. Tilden! I was never more glad to see anyone in my life!"

"And I was never more glad to see anyone in my life, either! I was afraid you were killed in this accident. Boy, if you had been, your cousin would have had my head!"

"Why would he blame you?" Kay asked.

"He sent me to Lake Diamond expressly to keep an eye on you, but you're a hard person to protect!" he said with a sigh.

"Quick, Ollie Desrale is down there. We've got to see if he's still alive," the girl cried, clutching at the bushes as she climbed down the snowy precipice to the wreck.

"See if who's alive?" Tilden asked as he followed her.

"Ollie Desrale. You know, one of the robbers!"

"Where did you find him?" the man gasped begrudgingly. He was somewhat resentful that Kay— and not he—had been the one to find the thief.

"I didn't find him. He found me," Kay panted, still picking her way down over icy rocks. "I didn't know it, but he was the driver of the sleigh I took to return to the hotel. He drove me out here and I jumped off just before he had the accident and went off the cliff!"

By this time Kay and Tilden had reached the crushed sleigh and whimpering horses.

"We'll have to put these horses out of their misery," Tilden sighed.

Kay looked away as the detective drew out his revolver.

"Wait!" she cried suddenly. "Let's look for Desrale first. He may be in the wreck!"

"If he hasn't made his getaway!" Tilden growled. "No! Here he is! Tangled up in the reins and badly injured."

The revolver went off twice. There was a moan, a brief thumping of heavy hoofs, then silence. Kay ventured to turn and look.

"That takes care of the horses, poor things," the detective sighed. "Now we can cut away the tangled leather and see to Desrale."

Desrale lay unconscious in a crumpled heap. It was a miracle that he was still alive.

"We can't get him up the cliff," the detective grunted. "We'd better leave him and go back for help."

"That could take too long. Let's take this seat cushion from the sleigh and rig up parts of the harness to it. Then we can pull Desrale up the hill on it."

"Not a bad idea," Tilden admitted with grudging admiration for Kay's ingenuity.

Together they made a make-shift stretcher for the wounded man then pulled him slowly and carefully to the top of the hill.

"Now to put him into my sleigh," the detective panted, exhausted from the difficult climb.

"He's coming to!" Kay said as Ollie, his eyes still

closed, began mumbling indistinctly. "He's trying to say something," she added, leaning nearer to catch the words.

"What's he saying?"

"Something about a Belden Apartment, I think. That is all I can make out."

"Listen carefully. He may give away some secrets," Tilden said.

XXIII

A Clue

The badly injured Desrale was taken to the Diamond Lake Hospital, and left there under a police guard.

In the meantime Wendy and Betty had gone back to the hotel hoping to find Kay.

"Where could she be?" Betty wondered. "I hope nothing's happened to her."

"You know Kay!" Wendy replied. "And you know anything is apt to happen to her! We're going to miss the train if she doesn't show up soon."

"There's Chris Eaton. Maybe she knows something about Kay," Betty suggested.

"I hate to ask that girl anything."

"Well, I will then!" Betty declared. "Hi, Chris! Have you seen Kay? We lost her in the crowd down by the lake awhile ago."

"I haven't been near the lake," Chris replied with a superior air. "I'm afraid I'm not the outdoors type particularly when there are so many more interesting ways to spend one's afternoon."

Her mysterious manner irritated Betty who asked tartly, "Well, and what was so interesting? I know you're dying to tell us!"

Chris tossed her head. "Sometimes you girls seem awfully young to me!" she said. "Personally I enjoy a little more sophisticated company!"

"And you were in sophisticated company this afternoon?" Wendy asked.

"I should say so! I met an absolutely fascinating woman. She's also extremely wealthy."

"What was so interesting about all that?" Betty asked crossly.

"Her jewelry! I mentioned how crazy I was about jewelry and she invited me over to see hers. They were like the jewels of a queen."

"Just tell us one thing, Chris. Have you seen Kay?" Betty asked.

Chris ignored the question and went on, "I told her that my aunt, Mrs. Pinty, collects jewelry. I asked if she was interested in seeing some of it. My aunt's jewelry is very beautiful and rare, you know."

"No, I didn't know," Betty said, and she added inwardly, "and I don't care! All I want to know is, 'Where is Kay?'"

"So what do you suppose I did?" Chris asked continuing her story.

"I have no idea," Wendy said, adding, "please just tell us if you've seen Kay?"

"No, I haven't," Chris said carelessly. "But just listen to this! I smuggled Auntie's jewels over to show this lady. Auntie would have a perfect fit if she knew I did it, but what she doesn't know won't hurt her!" the girl chuckled.

Neither Wendy nor Betty responded but Chris

rattled on anyway; "I wanted to show them to someone who would appreciate them."

"Tell me something," Betty interrupted, "how is it that you trusted this woman when you'd known her so short a time?"

"It isn't always the length of time that counts in knowing people. It's the compatibility one feels. Now as long as I've known you I've never felt you understood me and appreciated the same things I do. With this new friend something clicked at once and I realized that she and I had a lot in common."

"Well," Betty said, "I do hope your new friend didn't feel so appreciative of the jewelry that she kept it!"

"Just what are you insinuating?" Chris asked angrily.

"That you were very foolish to show your aunt's jewelry to some chance acquaintance!" Wendy replied bluntly.

"You don't know what you're talking about," Chris snapped.

"Well, did you get the jewelry back?" Betty asked.

"Why, of course! Don't be silly!" Chris retorted. "Here! See for yourself!"

She opened her purse and pulled out a small jewel case. Opening it she revealed several pieces lying on the white satin lining.

But they were not Mrs. Pinty's jewels! Winking up mockingly at the girls were cheap glass imitations!

"Oh, no!" wailed Chris, instantly realizing her foolishness and her loss.

"You've been tricked," Betty said.

"What can I do!" Chris cried, bursting into tears. "Here comes my aunt now! Oh, what can I do?"

"You'd better tell her the truth," Betty urged.

"I can't! I'm scared to death!"

"You have no choice!" Wendy said.

Mrs. Pinty spotted the three girls and noticed immediately that her niece was crying hysterically. The woman swept across the room and addressed the twins sharply.

"What have you two been saying to upset Chris? I cannot understand why you and that Tracey youngster always torment my poor niece! Speak up, Chris, and tell me what the trouble is!"

The twins said nothing, but eyed Chris intently.

"They haven't done anything, Auntie!" Chris sniffled. "I just don't feel well!"

The twins continued to look at Chris but they themselves said nothing. Their silence was more effective than a stream of words could be. Chris finally broke down, saying; "Oh, Auntie! I've done something terrible and you'll never forgive me, but I really didn't mean any harm!"

"What are you talking about?" the woman said irritably.

While Chris was making a clean confession, Kay appeared, accompanied by Mr. Tilden. Both looked disheveled and weary from their adventure on the mountainside.

"Oh good, you're back! Now you can help us," Betty cried. "You're just the two people we need!"

"Why, what's happened?" Kay asked.

Wendy hastily explained the situation, after which Kay introduced Tilden to Mrs. Pinty.

"Mr. Tilden is a detective. Just the person you need!"

The detective was assuring Mrs. Pinty of his aid, when Wendy noticed the time and interrupted.

"The last train back to Brantwood leaves in four minutes," she exclaimed.

"That means we can't go home tonight!" Betty panicked.

"Don't worry. I'll phone home and explain everything," Kay said. "They'll think it's all worthwhile when they hear the news!"

"What news?" the twins demanded. "Kay! What have you been up to? We've been so concerned about Chris that we forgot to ask you!"

"We've caught Ollie Desrale!" Kay announced proudly.

"Tell us all about it!"

"Let me phone home first."

Kay explained to her mother that Ollie had been caught; that the loss of Mrs. Pinty's jewels required immediate attention; and that the last train for the night had left.

She also assured her mother that Mrs. Pinty would act as their chaperone.

"Mr. Tilden will be here too," the girl added. "He wants to stick around and see if Jack Beardsley shows up."

"Well, just be careful, Kay," her mother pleaded.

"I will," the girl promised. "And we have a good bodyguard in Mr. Tilden, so don't worry! Please explain everything to Mrs. Worth."

The girls were given a nice room together, adjoining the one occupied by Chris and her aunt. They talked for hours and then Kay went to see Chris.

"Tell me about this woman who took the jewelry," she asked the sullen girl.

"All I can tell you is that she was young and blonde and very pleasant."

"What was her name?" Kay asked eagerly.

"Adele Cortiz."

Kay's eyes lit up. "Where does she live?" she asked eagerly.

As she answered, Kay thought instantly of the delirious mutterings of Ollie!

"Belden Apartments," was Chris's reply.

XXIV

Hidden Loot

"Now at last we can put two and two together!" Kay thought to herself when she was back in her room. "It's clear that Jack Beardsley is disguised as a woman and is busy swindling the rich people at this resort. Evidently he is staying at the Belden Apartments! I'm sure we can catch him now. I've got to get Mr. Tilden."

On the phone Kay found a note from the twins which read, "Have gone to watch the moonlight skating on the lake. Join us at the boathouse."

Kay tried to reach Tilden a number of times but each time the switchboard operator reported, "No answer, Miss."

"Just when we could catch the thief," Kay thought, "Tilden is nowhere to be found! Now what? I know, I'll get the twins and we'll go to the Belden Apartments ourselves!"

There was quite a crowd at the lake and it took Kay some time to find the twins. However, as they'd promised, they had stayed near the boat-house and eventually Kay found them.

"Quick, come with me," she said in a low tone. "I have something much more exciting to do than watch the skating!"

She squeezed an arm of each twin and excitedly dragged the girls out of the throng.

"Oh, Kay, what's up now?" Betty cried, seeing the Tracey girl's flushed face.

There was a hasty explanation.

After Kay had explained, Betty asked, "Do you think we ought to go there without Mr. Tilden?"

"Or without letting anyone know where we are going?" Wendy added.

"Well, let's keep an eye out for Mr. Tilden. We may see him," Kay urged.

The girls pushed through the crowd and hurried on toward the Belden.

"There it is!" Kay exclaimed, as they reached an imposing looking apartment building on an exclusive street.

The girls had just reached the entrance when a well-dressed young woman came out. There was something vaguely familiar about her.

"Jack in disguise," Kay whispered, nudging the twins.

Fortunately, Beardsley did not notice the girls. He stepped into a waiting taxi and they heard him say, "To the Diamond Lake Hospital."

Just then Betty spotted Tilden. The detective stepped from the shadows and into another taxi. "Follow that car!" he said.

His driver shot off in hot pursuit.

"He was right on the job after all!" Kay cried. "And now that both Jack and Ollie are out of the way, let's search their apartment," she said entering the lobby.

"But how will we get in?" Wendy asked.

"Leave it to me," Kay whispered.

She went to the superintendent's desk and asked for "Miss Adele Cortiz."

"Sorry, Miss, but she has just gone out."

"Oh, dear!" the girl lamented. "What a shame! We've come such a long way to see her! It's really very important, too. How disappointing!"

"That's too bad!" the man said. "But I'm afraid I can't help you out."

"Couldn't we just run up and wait in her apartment?" Kay asked. "I assure you it would be alright with her."

Scrutinizing the girls, the superintendent could see that they were well-bred and most certainly trustworthy. He finally replied, "I guess, since you are friends of hers, it will be all right for you to go up and wait." He gave a key to the elevator boy, saying, "Take these young ladies up to the Cortiz apartment."

Up went the conspirators, trying to avoid each other's eyes for fear of giving way to a telltale giggle. The boy unlocked the door of the deserted apartment and in walked the young sleuths!

"As easy as that!" Betty said as the door was closed.

"Are you sure nobody is in here?" Wendy whispered nervously, but a quick check of the luxurious apartment showed it to be empty.

"To think those men live like this, while they rob people like poor Mrs. Dale who has to struggle with her half starved children!" Wendy exclaimed indignantly, as she looked around.

"Hurry up, let's see if we can find some of the loot," Kay suggested.

"A good joke on Miss Adele Cortiz if we do!" Betty said, beginning to hunt. "It'd be great to have her return and find her booty gone!"

The girls made a thorough search of every conceivable hiding place.

"Look here!" Kay called, her voice trembling with excitement.

Tucked in a bureau drawer as if they were the rightful belongings of the tenant, were leather jewel boxes filled with jewelry.

"Some of these must be Mrs. Pinty's," Wendy said.

"I'll say!" Kay exulted. "Look, this ring even has her name engraved in it."

"They've tried to scratch off the letters on other pieces but they're still readable!" Kay said.

The girls continued looking and pretty soon Betty called out, "I've found it!"

"Found what?" Kay demanded eagerly.

"Sh! Someone might hear us!" Wendy said nervously.

Betty produced a heavy manila envelope marked, "Cash and Securities of Mrs. Theodore Dale."

"How wonderful!" Wendy said.

"This is certainly the Dales' lucky day!" laughed Kay.

She now worked systematically in her search to find some trace of Miss Janey's loss, the purse and the suitcase.

"They can't be in the apartment," she declared, "because I've looked in every nook and cranny and there isn't a spot left big enough to hide them."

"Maybe Beardsley took out the valuables and threw the bags away," Wendy suggested.

"He must have," Kay agreed. "Now where—" Her eyes ran swiftly over possible hiding places. "Oh, why didn't I think of that before?"

Quickly the girl snatched off the covers from a bed and shook them. Then she lifted up one side of the mattress. There, well hidden, lay papers strapped together with thick elastic bands. Kay spread these sheets out to examine them.

"I can't believe it!" she shouted.

"Sh! Don't make so much noise!" Wendy whispered from the kitchen where she was busily looking for loot.

"I've actually found Miss Janey's formula!" Kay blurted out.

"And this must be the rest of her things," Betty added, delving into the package.

"Quick! Tear open that other bed!" Kay urged.

"Wouldn't it be awful if Beardsley came back and caught us doing this?" Betty said, as she jerked at sheets and blankets.

The other bed revealed nothing but at this moment Wendy who was looking through the kitchen shelves, gave a cry.

"I've found something!"

The girl had dumped out the contents from containers labeled "Flour," "Sugar," "Coffee," "Tea," "Salt," and "Spice," and the most surprising objects had spilled out.

"What are those things?" Betty asked.

"Things that were hidden in these containers!" Wendy cried. "Here's an old watch!"

She dusted off the flour that covered it and wiped the case clean. "There seems to be some engraving on it."

"Let's see!" Kay said, reaching for the watch. "Why, I know this watch! It's one the robbers stole from a train passenger in that holdup!"

"How can you tell?" Betty asked.

"It says Richard Birdsong on it!" Kay replied. "It was such an odd name it stuck in my memory. I remember hearing the man talk about it and thinking what a strange name it was."

"What else have you found?" Betty asked, as Wendy plunged her hand into the sugar and felt all around, finally uncovering a beautiful sapphire ring.

"Ella Eaton's ring!" Kay exclaimed. "What a fuss she made about it!"

"Quiet!" Wendy whispered. "What was that?"

The three girls froze. Wendy poised on a kitchen chair, remained motionless, one hand holding a spice box in mid-air!

A key was being rattled in the lock. The front door swung open!

"Quick, hide!" Betty whispered in a panic.

Wendy slipped quietly from her chair and tiptoed into the pantry closet. Betty and Kay crowded frantically in on top of her. Softly Kay closed the door.

Heavy footsteps resounded across the polished floor of the living room. The girls had left the things they had discovered on the library table.

"He'll find those things and all the mess we've made and know somebody has been here!" Betty whispered into Kay's ear.

"Now he's coming into the kitchen!"

In her panic Wendy knocked over a pan but luckily Kay was able to catch it before it crashed to the floor. Then came the scuff of footsteps across the kitchen linoleum.

"What's all this?" a man's voice muttered.

Evidently he had seen the spilled flour, sugar, tea and coffee, and the articles the girls had dropped as they had leaped into their hiding place.

"Well, this is a nice haul!" the man said to himself.

"It can't be Beardsley!" Betty breathed.

The man marched to and fro, then went into the

living room. After what seemed like ages there was the sound of the front door creaking open again and banging shut. Then complete silence.

"He's gone!" Kay said, opening the pantry door a crack and peeking out.

"Let's get out of here!" Betty said urgently.

"All those things are gone except the Birdsong watch which I slipped into my pocket, and the sapphire ring I had on my finger!" Kay cried.

The money, securities and jewels were gone.

"How infuriating!" Wendy cried.

"I can't believe we actually found the Janey formula, only to have it whisked away again the next minute!" Kay groaned.

"Let's get out of here before we're caught!" Wendy begged.

The three girls cautiously opened the hall door and stepped out of the apartment.

"Hands up!" thundered a man's voice!

XXV

Happiness

The startled girls flung their arms over their heads and froze. Wendy had turned white, Betty was trembling, but Kay burst out laughing.

"Oh, Mr. Tilden!" she cried, dropping her arms. "You gave us such a fright!"

"Sorry if I really scared you," the detective said, smiling, "but I had to have my little joke! You girls will beat me at my own business if I'm not careful. I see you unearthed the loot!"

"I can't believe we found it all!" Kay exulted.

"The last we saw of you, Mr. Tilden, was when you jumped in the taxi and chased Beardsley. He was dressed up as Adele Cortiz," Betty said.

"Oh, did you see me go?" He laughed. "You girls don't miss a thing, do you?"

"We heard Cortiz tell the driver to go to the hospital and we heard you tell the driver to follow!"

"Yes, we got to the hospital at about the same time," Tilden reported. "I waited until our friend was actually inside Desrale's room. You remember we had a police guard there. They arrested the disguised Beardsley right at Ollie's bedside. It worked out very neatly!" A wide grin lit up the detective's face.

"Good for you!" Kay said.

"Then what did you do?" Betty asked.

"I came straight back here to search the apartment. I suspected that the loot might be hidden here, just as you did. And I also suspected you were here!"

"How did you know that?" Wendy asked.

"I gathered from the description given me by the superintendent downstairs that the three girls he let in the Cortiz apartment were you assistant sleuths!"

"That superintendent is going to be surprised when he finds out what has been going on right in this building," said Kay.

"We'd better go and break the news to him," Tilden answered, pressing the bell for the elevator.

"To think such scoundrels were living right here in my building!" was the superintendent's reaction. "We've always been so careful to keep a good class of tenants! I hope this doesn't ruin the Belden Apartments' reputation!"

"How did they manage to keep their cover?" Kay asked.

"Why, there was nothing the least bit suspicious about them. They were a quiet couple, the man and the one I took for his sister. I never imagined that young woman was a fake! They were so quiet, easy to please, and so inconspicuous I never noticed much about them!"

"Well, they are both going to a place where they'll be even less conspicuous," Tilden assured him with a satisfied smile.

"We ought to get back to the hotel!" Kay said. "It's pretty late and poor Mrs. Pinty will be wondering where we are! Besides, I can hardly wait to see her face when we return her jewelry!"

"We'd better keep close to Mr. Tilden and let him guard those valuables, I wouldn't want them to be stolen again!" Wendy said.

"Don't worry, I'll get you and the gems back to Mrs. Pinty safe and sound," the detective promised.

This he did, and the girls went immediately to Mrs. Pinty's room. Mrs. Pinty was furious at them for going off without letting her know.

"Just a minute," Kay said. "We have something here which may excuse our staying out so late. I apologize for upsetting you but I think this will make you feel that we were justified."

Before the woman could launch into another outburst, Kay handed her the jewels. Like the sun breaking through storm clouds came a smile across Mrs. Pinty's face!

"Why—what—where!" she stammered in amazement.Seeing the valuables which had been lost through her own folly, she gave a cry of relief.

"How did you do it?" exclaimed the happy woman. "I never expected to lay eyes on these again! You cannot imagine what this means to me!"

Kay rapidly outlined the story of the thieves and their double disguise.

"Why, that's an amazing story!" cried the woman. "Chris, don't you think it's simply marvelous the way they traced the criminals and recovered all these stolen things?"

In response Chris ungraciously mumbled something about not knowing Miss Cortiz was a man in disguise.

Kay and the twins went on to tell about finding other loot in the apartment, including the sapphire ring stolen from Chris's cousin, Ella Eaton.

"I know it's not a laughing matter but I can't help smiling when I think of that dreadful man masquerading as a woman!" Mrs. Pinty remarked.

"I can hardly wait to get back to Brantwood and tell everybody our adventures!" Chris twittered, the high spirits of the group finally dispelling her usual sourness toward her classmates.

The next morning they all took the first train back to Brantwood. The twins and Kay promptly set out to return the stolen items to their rightful owners.

"I think we should go to the Dales' first," Kay said.

"Good idea," Wendy said. "This money is going to make such a change in their lives."

"They're all out in front of the house," Betty added as Kay stopped the car at the Dales' gate. "And look who's with them! Nanna herself!"

"Seeing the way she is with the children makes me understand why Mrs. Dale always speaks so warmly of her. She is an entirely different person from the old witch we thought she was!" Kay added.

Seeing the girls approach, the children scampered to greet them.

"Did you bring any more chocolate cake?" one boy asked.

"No, not this time," Kay laughed, "but I have something else which I think you'll all like even better than cake!"

"What is it? What is it?" clamored the children.

With a smile Kay handed over the stolen inheritance to Teddy.

"Here you are," she said. "You've tried so hard to get back your mother's money that I think you ought to be the one to return it to her!"

Teddy could hardly believe his eyes. With a whoop of joy he raced to his mother.

"Look, look, mother! We have Daddy's money back again, we won't be poor any more!"

"How did you ever, ever do it?" she gasped.

Kay and the twins gave a vivid account of all their adventures in chasing the robbers and in learning of the double disguise. The whole group was spellbound by the story. As for Nanna, she was greatly perturbed at the account of the train robber who had dressed himself up to look like her.

"Why, people must think I'm in cahoots with them!" she exclaimed.

"I'm afraid we thought so ourselves, for a while," Kay confessed.

"I'll be very careful about who lives in my house after this!" the old woman vowed.

Beyond that she didn't say a word remaining as much a figure of mystery as ever!

"We really should be getting along to Miss Janey's now," Kay said. "Goodbye, Mrs. Dale, and good luck!"

After profuse thanks from the widow the girls drove to Miss Janey's home. A familiar car stood in front of the house.

"Doctor Staunton seems to be visiting again!" Kay laughed.

"I think they're in love," Wendy said.

Relishing the thought the girls smiled as they hurried up the front steps.

"That other gentleman's in there and your cousin, too, Miss Tracey," Jessie whispered, as she greeted the girls at the door. "Doctor Staunton brought them. They've all been talking science!"

Wondering who the "other gentleman" was the girls moved quietly toward the living room door. There sat Gus Fearson, deep in conversation with Doctor Staunton. Bill was talking to Miss Janey.

"Perhaps you won't need your old formula now," Kay interrupted impulsively, "but here it is!"

"And here are all the other things you lost when your bag and suitcase were stolen!" Betty burst out.

"What do you mean?" Miss Janey gasped.

"How wonderful! It's simply amazing!" Miss Janey exclaimed after the girls had relayed the story.

"Good work, Kay!" Bill said, smiling proudly.

"Well, well! You students certainly deserve a high mark in detective work as well as in chemistry!" Doctor Staunton praised.

"Miss Janey has been good enough to recommend me to the company that is buying the patent," Gus Fearson explained happily as he got up to leave.

The girls were delighted that everything was turning out so well.

"I can hardly believe that I am so happy today, when only a short time ago I was so miserable!" Miss Janey sighed. "Kay you've been wonderful from the very beginning!" Then blushingly she added, "I think you should be the first one to know a little secret. Doctor Staunton and I are to be married in the spring!"

This news was the perfect end to their adventure and it was only after much hugging and congratulating that the girls finally left.

"What a winter this has been!" Wendy said as they drove to town. "A robbery, a den of thieves, swindling, an old witch——"

"A train holdup!" Kay said, "and a fall over the mountainside——"

"Capturing the thieves," Betty added.

"And recovering the loot," Wendy said with satisfaction.

"And through it all," Kay Tracey laughed, "the mystery of the Double Disguise!"

"What next?" wondered the twins.